The Hater's Prayer

By C. Marie Evans

C. Marie Evans

THE HATER'S PRAYER

Midwest Creations Publishing Titles
By C. Marie Evans
(Pseudonym of Author Chantay M. James)

Afro-Romance Series
The Hater's Prayer

By Author under Chantay M. James

The Brainwaiver Series
Waivering Minds
Waivering Lies
Waivering Winds (Novella)

Other titles:
Valley of Decisions
(Xulon Press, 2005)
(Midwest Creations Publishing, 2017)

Anthologies featuring the Author:
A Hawk's Tale
(KDP) Electronic Version (MOBI)
----Author Alias: Chantay Hadley---
(*with P. Lee, D. Outlaw and A. Johnson*)

Title Page:
A Hater's Prayer
C. Marie Evans
Midwest Creations Publishing

Midwest Creations Publishing
Faith-Based Fiction

Midwest Creations Publishing
St. Louis, MO 63138
Visit our website at https://midwest-creations-publishing.square.site

A Hater's Prayer.

Edited by Midwest Creations Publishing
Designed by Midwest Creations Publishing
Scripture quotations are taken from the Complete Jewish Bible.
Printed in the United States of America

Originally published electronically via KDP by Midwest Creations Publishing

In Memory of Eunice Evans. You are gone, but not forgotten. The one true Annie B., we are your legacy. And we will go on to make you proud. Love you, Mama. And miss you so very much.

Chapter 1

"Yo. My name is Naomi Brooks, I'm 34 years old and I hate my sister. Well. Not HATE hate, like Jews hate Hitler or models hate weight gain, but like, love-hate... Like, I could really get down with some pineapple upside down cake if I just took the pineapples off. But because I don't feel like going through all that, I just settle on not eating it period. And, for the record, I like pineapples and I like cake; I just don't like them TOGETHER.

And no, my sister isn't some evil cheerleader type from high school that bullied me ever since we were kids, or some know it all that always corrected my grammar growing up. In fact, had our lives turned out a little differently, I'd actually think she was kind of cool."

"She still a stuck-up heifer tho!"

"Ignore that. That's my best friend Charmaine Reynolds, or Maine as we like to call her. She's a hater too, at least where my sister is concerned. Ever since Destiny (that's my sister – awesome name, right?) showed up at church with Maine's "undeclared crush" Michael Wallace two years ago – a guy she's been in love with since we were twelve y'all – she has declared Destiny Brooks the Wicked Witch of West St. Louis County.

While I can't aspire to quite that level of petty, to be real, I don't like how I feel. Let me explain: I don't like faking the big bouncy hugs that I must suffer through once a month at Big Mama's house. And I really don't like the plastic smiles that I must wear when hearing about Destiny's latest accomplishment from my stepmom, Brenda."

"Oh, did I tell you that Destiny won the Boardwalk Magazine nomination for Journalist of the year?" or, "Oh Nahmi (that's my nickname – only Dad used to call me that), you should have SEEN your sister go! This is the third year in a row that she has qualified in the State competition for the 400-meter dash. Isn't that magnificent?" or "Nahmi! Don't forget to call your sister this weekend and pray with her. She's being sent over to Dubai to cover that woman on trial for killing the man that tried to rape her. This could win your sister a Pulitzer!"

"And I don't like hating fulfilling my obligatory, sister-date night. The night of whenever my sister is home from covering some awesome assignment over in cat-man-wherever and she calls me to "catch up" and "hang out." It's those nights that I hate the most. And I bet you're thinking that I'm some drama queen, spoiled younger sibling that wanted Daddy all to myself. Well, you're right. And wrong. Here's why:

My mother and father, Rebecca and Daniel Brooks, met and fell in love near Cardinal Ritter

High School at just sixteen years old. They had sex (hello me) and got married (because Grandad Joshua did NOT play) and finished high school raising me before taking college courses and working full time jobs – because Big Mama didn't play.

And while mom and dad are both tall at 5'10 and 6'3, mom has always been what they call "thick" whereas dad had remained slim and muscular due to his love of basketball. So, though I inherited Dad's height (I settled nicely at 6'1") and his love of basketball, I also inherited mom's thickness and shade of skin (redbone to some, cinnamon to others) along with moms thick and difficult to train hair.

My childhood wasn't unhappy. I had two young, hard working parents that lived with my grandparents early on. Life wasn't a fairy tale then, but it was close. Because my grandparents were the BEST. Grandpa Joshua was a Deacon at Mt. Beulah Missionary Baptist Church and a contractor that owned his own business. Big Mama was the grandma that most folks see on tv, the best soul food you could eat every weekend and an awesome mother of 6 (Dad being the youngest) thus grandmother to many, making all that joy look effortless.

That meant I had my cousins, aunts, uncles and family surrounding me with love, attention and approval up until we moved out when I was four.

Mom and Dad bought their first house together in University City on Pershall Road, near North and South Avenue. I loved that house. I had my own room (of course) with no cousins to work my nerves and no Aunts always keeping that one eye on me, constantly catching me "up to no good".

I made friends, played hard and life was... well, it was okay. Because I'd missed my cousins and I'd missed my aunts; but mostly, I missed my Grandparents.

My mom's parents, Jeff and Maurine Slater had divorced long before I was born. Consequently, Mom rarely saw Poppa Jeff, a state of being that was passed down to me. Granny – that's Grandma Maurine, however, visited a lot. A whole lot. And she probably shouldn't have. Had she visited less, it would be safe to assume that my Dad and Mom would still be married. Granny was a wild one. A drinker, smoker (of weed mostly) and a partier to her name, Granny was always about being lit. Unfortunately, her life goal of lit-ness almost killed me when I was six. She was drinking and driving. And babysitting.

It had been the last straw for Dad, but not the only one. I was too young to remember what the arguments were about, but I remember them well. I also remember Dad hitting Mom once and Mom pulling the gun out of her drawer. She told Daddy that if he ever put his hands on her again, she'd send his black blip-blip-blippity blip (that's how I'd described it to Big Mama) to see Jesus up front and personal. Peaking around their door frame, I'd seen a look of such resolve on my Mama's face. She'd meant what she said. And when she cocked the gun to prove her point, I silently ran to the kitchen to hide between the wall and the fridge. Don't judge me. And don't ask me why, it seemed like a good idea at the time.

I didn't want to watch my Daddy die. But I didn't know how to feel about him hitting her either. Part of me felt like he asked for it. My Dad was supposed to be our protector. And while he would say that often, that was never something Mama really needed. She tended to lean on herself when it came to protection. She taught herself how to handle and fire a gun (and me also once I turned sixteen), she taught herself how to fight, attended self-defense classes and knew various types of martial arts. That's right. My mama was a bad ass.

I think it was Mom's self-sufficiency that put a wedge between her and Dad. Dad was raised in the Church. A man handled the protection. A man was the head of his home. A man was the main provider.

But Mom grew up with a weed smoking partier that was mostly a single parent. Poppa Jeff sometimes brought money by or took Mom to family reunions then not turn up for another three years or so, but Granny was the main parental influence in Mom's life.

So, Mom practically raised herself. She learned to cook so she wouldn't be eating White Castle's or Chinese food for dinner every night. She learned to fight so when the entire Goodman family (that's four sisters and two brothers) tried to jump her on the Hodiamont tracks (a narrow back street in St. Louis City) for her lunch money, she met them with bricks, stick's, trashcan lids and broken bottles. And won.

And when she met my dad, it's because she'd almost run him over on Vandeventer Avenue, coming from a friend's football game at Cardinal Ritter High School, teaching herself how to drive in that same friend's car.

My mom has never been the sort to wait for her Prince Charming to come. She saved herself. Often. And raised me to do the same.

But my Dad was THE Prince Charming. He was the romantic, sweep you off your feet and dance you into the ground kind of guy. My mom was the practical, I can walk myself thank you and, let's dance but be mindful of the time because we have to work in the morning – kind of girl.

Dad would jokingly call her a buzzkill or boring sometimes, never seeing how the light would flicker, then dim in her eyes. Because unlike Mom, he'd never gone to bed hungry. He'd never been left with a house full of relatives that he barely knew and sometimes an uncle that couldn't keep his hands to himself.

Dad never worried about what he was going to eat or who he was going to be. He had Big Mama speaking God's word into his life and Grandpa Joshua speaking God's word over it. He was taught how to be a man by loving parents.

Mama had herself. And only herself. Until she was sixteen and got a taste of what true parenting looked like from Dad's parents. Which was probably why Mom and Dad co-parented rather easily and possibly the very factor that attributed to my lack of breaking down after their divorce. Big Mama and Grandpa Joshua were just as much Mom's parents as they were Dad's. Meaning, life barely changed for me, aside from my parents now living in separate houses.

Until Dad met her. Brenda. Brenda Elizabeth Holland. To me, also known as, the Fairy Princess. I called her that because that's what she looked like. She was tiny and perfectly shaped, blonde and bubbly, she was uber friendly and always smiling.

I wanted to hate her. But Mom loved her! Big Mama loved her! My aunts (who wanted to hate her because she was white) couldn't hold out for long either, the woman was just that lovable! I even played the brat game, something that not only did NOT work, but got my butt whooped by Mom AND Dad (yeah, never played that game again). The only person that wasn't all the way won over was Grandpa Joshua, and even he began to thaw by the time they were married.

Which they were on March 17th (yes, St. Patrick's Day), four days after my seventh birthday. It was an event that led to one of the best years of my life as I remember it. I had TWO moms, two homes and two times EVERYTHING I ever wanted. I'm not saying that I can be bought, but I am saying that seven-year-old me had no problem with that concept. Technically I'd gotten an extra mom for my birthday, so life was good.

What I hadn't counted on however, was my birthday present the following year. A baby sister. My baby sister. Something I hadn't even realized was happening until Dad and I were sitting in the waiting room in DePaul hospital. It was Big Mama who asked me how I felt about getting a new sister or brother that shined the headlights right into my doe-like horrified, light-stricken gaze.

But I recovered quickly. Like my mom, I was all about survival – so I ushered myself into the unknown by lifting up a prayer for a baby brother. I'd always secretly wanted a brother. I remember how excited I was at the concept of a little version of dad running around the house with me, following me, learning from his big sis.

"It's a girl!"

Someone had shouted it, but I'd refused to believe it. Surely the God my family loved and served wouldn't be so callous as to completely ignore my request for a brother? I mean, I realized the prayer had come in at the last minute but, technically, that wasn't my fault since I'd just found out. And God was God, right? I mean, He should have already known what I would want because He was God and Big Mama said He knew everything.

So, what's the deal with this sister junk? Yep. I remember thinking all of that. I thought it that night in the waiting room while my relatives danced, laughed and high fived around me. I'd thought it in my room three nights later when Dad brought Brenda and the baby home for the first time. And I'd thought it that very next day when Brenda taught me how to hold my newborn baby sister who was wrapped up in pink and yellow blankets, looking all pasty and pink with a huge bow around her bald head.

And so what, she was kind of cute and looked like one of my baby dolls (that I never played with because they creeped me out a little). And so what, she opened her eyes, blinked at me then reached up and grabbed hold of my finger, blew a spit bubble and wouldn't let go. Ugh. The girl was giving me death grip hugs even then.

"Her name is Destiny, Nahmi. Isn't she gorgeous?" I couldn't lie. Well, I could have, but it wouldn't have changed the truth. She WAS gorgeous. She was beautiful. She was all that was pure and right and light in the world. And the precursor of my future.

From that moment on, it was, "Look at Destiny! Isn't she smart?" or "Isn't she pretty," or "Isn't she a genius?"

The only break in routine from the Destiny, Destiny, Destiny in my life came five years after her birth when Dad was killed by a stray bullet downtown; handing out food to the homeless near Memorial park, no less.

On that day I held my sister tucked tight into my left side and shielding her as best I could from a reality we would both have to eventually face. A life once colored in all the hues of a rainbow had, just that quickly, grayed into shades of light and shadow; until there was nothing left but an overcast, stormy sky.

Hugging me tight with her face buried in my side, I knew Destiny didn't really understand what dead meant. But I knew my sister. She didn't understand what was wrong, but she knew, as she stood there gripping me and shaking like a leaf, that something definitely was. She felt the loss, just like I did. And the pain surrounding her as the adults in the room dealt with that loss in various ways, she read it and instinctively knew, that she should fear it.

Unable to stand another second of it, I took the first of many steps toward the rear dining room door that led to Big Mama's kitchen. Once there, I hefted Destiny up onto the table before going over to Big Mama's kitchen counter; I grabbed and hauled over to sit beside her the Big Deal cookie Jar. That was what Big Mama called it. It was a huge cookie jar, filled with all types of the best, homemade cookies you could ever eat. Big Mama always kept it full and was always ready to pull it out for her grandkids, especially whenever they brought her news of some small achievement. To everyone else, it was small, but to Big Mama, it was a big deal, thus the name. Because a big deal like whatever news we'd dropped for her approval deserved a "big deal" reward.

Before I opened the jar though, I shoved my baby sister's hand's off her face, grabbed a napkin and patted away the tears. She sniffled and blinked at me, her little pink pout shaking.

"Don't cry, Dessy. Okay?"

She nodded and gripped her hands tight in her lap, but I could see the tears refilling again.

"Come on kid. Don't cry. I got the cookie jar right here. If you stop crying, it's a big deal. And you know what that means, right?"

"I get a cookie?" She said, her five-year-old shaky "trying not to cry" voice nearly breaking me.

"Yeah. Yeah, girl, you get a cookie. See?" I hurried to pull the lid off, fighting tears of my own. My Daddy was gone. How could that even happen? I shook off those thoughts and grabbed the first cookie I could. Luckily it was her favorite and mine, chocolate chip.

The trembly smile that hit her baby pout at the sight of the cookie came and went in an instant, so quick I almost missed it.

"I want Daddy, Nahmi." And there went the tears. "Where is Daddy? Where did he go, Nahmi?"

I'd dropped the cookie and the lid to pull my little sister over to me, hugging her close so she could rest her head on my shoulder, the same way I used to when I could carry her around when she was two.

"Daddy is with Jesus now Dessy. God took him." I don't know if I'd believed it when I said it. I'd heard Big Mama say that earlier and it seemed like the right thing to say.

"Why Nahmi? Why Jesus take our Daddy? When is he coming home?"

She was crying then. And so was I. Because I had no answer to that. Which was what I said.

On that day, she wasn't just Destiny and I wasn't just Naomi. On that day we were sisters, lost in our grief over a concept that we couldn't possibly fathom. And while it had been the worst day ever, the burst of love for my sister born that day had to be the very love that keeps me from Hating-hating her, that powers my fake bouncy hugs and adds brightness to my fake-proud smiles. Because while they might be mostly fake, there's a teeny tiny bit of real to them; a dichotomy that confuses me just as much as I'm sure it's confusing you.

And is exactly what brought on my and Charmaine's invention; the Web-zine and podcast currently blowing up all over the nation, Hater-cation for the Hater-Nation: An end result that I'm weirdly proud of, from us reciting twice a day, every day for two years, The Hater's Prayer."

Chapter 2

"Now, before we get into that, I told you a little bit about my sister including how cute she was back in the day. But here's the current day bio of one, Destiny Marie Brooks engaged to one, Michael Anthony Wallace (the current Prince Charming on the block and runner-up only to Dad regarding handsomeness).

At twenty-six, my sister has become the most accomplished Journalist of her time. Not only is she smart, sweet and funny; she is STUNNING. Okay, I am not exaggerating when I say this because I mean exactly what I say, she is stunning with a capital STUN."

"And STILL a stuck-up heifer!"

"Charmaine! Will you STOP!"

"I'm just saying!"

"Don't! Don't just say. Interrupt again and I'm sending you to your corner!"

"And that, best friend, is why you suck!"

Deep, calm breath.

Anyway, like I was saying, my sister makes models look like starved, bitter waifs, barely tolerated by a camera that should love them versus beat them into submission.

Her hair has always been perfect, long and soft, full of burnished red-brown curls. Hanging past her shoulders to mid-back, she just washes and conditions it, slaps on a headband right out of the shower, a bit of mousse for hold and

BAM. She's done. A hair-do so perfect, she only needs a visit to her stylist every two weeks for shaping and one or two highlights a year, if that.

Standing at 5'6, my sister has a way of combining Dad's confident and easy stride with her mom's fairy light, whimsy exuberance; she dang near brings joy and bounce every time she enters a room.

Her eyes are a hazel in a blue-green kind of way that changes colors with her moods ranging from happy to really happy to concentration… and back to happy.

And you wouldn't be able to tell by looking at her straight, gorgeous white teeth that she barely needed a retainer to align them; unlike my full mouth of metal that ran its gauntlet of embarrassment a full three years.

Let's do the comparison, shall we? My sister, the biracial epitome of beauty (and the go-to standard of all people famous these days) stood at mid height, slim with a perfect shape (like her mom), beautiful eyes and hair, a breathtaking spirit of joy and a smile that would put every dentist commercial actor to shame.

And then there's me. Tall at 6'1 with skin a caramel crème shade, my "thick" gave way to what is cutely termed these days as "plus-sized" at a size eighteen waist, with regular brown eyes, a reddish-brown, z-patterned curl (that's nappy) fro that puts me at 6'2 (thank goodness for my slim neck and the slimming factor of big hair), I possess a somewhat disgruntled spirit and still retain a slight overbite despite my many years in braces, giving my smile a goofy, horse-grin quality.

Yeah. And you wondered why I sort a hate my sister.

"Do me!"

"Maine!"

"Do me! Do me Domedomedomedome!!!"

"Okay! Jeez! For our podcast audience out there, that haven't seen any of our spots on YouTube, Maine, like me is plus sized – but only because she has hips and a behind the size of a small Honda..."

"Hey!"

"You asked for it, and don't interrupt, please. Like I was saying, hippy with booty galore, my bestie also wears a size 18 so the plus moniker fits, she stands at about 5 feet and 9 inches and possesses glorious blond locks down to the middle of her back. Her eyes also an uninspiring brown like mine..."

"Really?"

"Hush. Where was I? Oh, uninspiring eyes like mine, at least the Creator saw fit to give them long, gorgeous lashes and an almond shape, the girl will never have a need for mascara, eyeliner or eye-makeup, her eyes are just that perfect."

"Aw, thanks bestie."

"You're welcome. Now shut it."

"Red fsd hfffrr...."

"What?"

"Nothing."

"Hashtag eyeroll. Anyway, like I was saying, for like, the eightieth time, Maine and I are pretty much the sistas that hung out on the porch of that old show 227 whereas my sister is like Sandra (the actress was Jacquee Harry I think) all beautiful, gorgeous and just plain... awesome.

So. For the listener that emailed us the question of how Hater-cation for the Hater-nation got started, that is your answer. Because as Christians we're not supposed to envy our neighbors or covet what they have. It's wrong and we know it. But how do we NOT do that? When some people seem to be born with everything they could ever want?

Check it, here's what I'm talking about. I've always wanted to be a writer. But practicality states that there isn't any money in that unless you're Stephen King. So, what did I do? I got my Bachelor of Arts in Business at Webster University and went on to work for the State of Missouri in the Children's Division. Oh, joy.

My sister? Destiny didn't have a clue what she wanted to do. She was asked to write an article for the school paper at Ladue Horton-Watkins, her high school when she was a sophomore. She wrote the article and found that she enjoyed it. Her advisor sent the article to the Post-Dispatch as an admission for some contest. She won. And kept winning. Until she won a scholarship – a full ride - to Purdue University.

I played basketball in high school and was pretty good. I had some all-conference and a few division awards. My team even took the state championship home my senior year. My sister? Excelling in track in the 400-meter dash and the whatever meter it is (I just remember it was one lap) relay, was a state qualifier all four years in high school. While I graduated with nine letters, she graduated with twelve.

My sophomore year, I was homecoming queen. My sister was homecoming queen her freshmen and sophomore year and prom queen her junior and senior year.

I had one best friend and a few people I consider friends that happen to be coworkers.

My sister has friends everywhere, and I mean EVERYWHERE. We cannot step into a store, a restaurant or even a gas station without someone there knowing (and loving) my sister.

And last but not least, at our church, I'm practically snubbed, while my sister is seen as the golden child. But that's not her fault. Both of us have somewhat followed in our mothers' footsteps.

While my sister finished her degree and started her career before starting a family; I met, fell in love with and married my soon to be ex-husband Rodney Carmichael. Because Grandpa Joshua STILL didn't play back then, that marriage took place when I was 19 years old (my freshman year in college) and pregnant with Connie B., my now, sixteen-year-old daughter. A daughter that wants to be JUST LIKE her aunt Destiny.

But unlike my parents, I held on to a marriage that was doomed to fail. And to this day, I still have no idea why. I don't know if it was to please a church full of folks that saw me as the family black sheep, or if it was to give my other two children, Madison Lacey (10) and Daniel Charles (3) the time with their father in the home that I would have appreciated as a kid.

Whatever the case, bottom line? I love my sister. But I hate how perfect she is. I hate how perfectly her life has been while I still work at a dead-end state job, barely scrape by and am about to be a divorced mother of three.

Which brings me back to what Maine and I call, the hater's prayer. And I will happily share that with you... on next week's podcast because we are so out of time! And hey, before you slam us in the comments for this cliffhanger, share this podcast on Facebook, Instagram and Twitter to tell your friends about how much we suck, THEN slam us in the comments. We love ya'll, catch you next week and remember; today's hater is tomorrows achiever! Use that fire in your belly to be great, the hate is just bait and..."

"There is no future but the fate we make!"

"Thank you, Terminator 2."

"Heifer."
"And we're out. Peace!"

"Alright ladies, that's a wrap. Good one."

My smile was so wide you could drive a hummer through it, so I just nodded at Vic and removed the headphones from my ears. Casting from the Radio 100 radio station where our friends Vic and Tony worked the night shift was always fun.

Fun because A, Tony had the biggest crush on Maine. But he was short, standing at about 5 feet 6 inches and Maine didn't even SEE short men (as in men her height or shorter). It was like he didn't exist as a man to her. Tony would run up, grab whatever she was carrying out of her hands, carry it for her and gush all over her to the point of disgusting. And Maine would smile, laugh, give him a hug and stop just short of patting his head, treat him like the little brother she always never wanted.

And B, because Vic was like, the guru of all things media and managed the AV and media outreach at church. When Maine and I'd approached him after service to ask him how we'd go about doing a podcast, he jumped at the opportunity to teach us the ropes. He brought us here to the Radio 100 station for our very first podcast a year ago as of tomorrow.

And C, Vic was good to look at. And by good, I mean, Tyler-Perry-movie good. Taller than me at around 6 feet 5, Vic was built like the pro football player he used to be. Dark brown eyes and head shaved clean; his chocolate brown muscles glowed with a sheen I couldn't identify. I wish that were all it was to him. Then maybe I wouldn't find him so fascinating lately, something that was also strange since we'd been friends even as little kids.

There was this one thing that was my downfall. He smelled really good. I don't mean like, cologne or Axe body spray good. I mean like Cool Water mixed with Captain America, Thor, Aqua Man and a touch of Vin Diesel, all mixed into a vat of sexy-man-after-a-shower smell.

This might be the reason I dropped the headphones and almost fell (twice) over the chairs between me and the door as he rounded the table to grab up the equipment we'd used.

Giving me a weird look that basically said, "I should ask why, but I don't think I really want to know," he chuckled before grabbing the headphones I'd just flung before heading back toward the door.

So, caught up in watching him leave, something I loved doing, I almost missed Maine's cackle.

I wanted to tell her to shut it again, but it would be pointless. Because she didn't get it no matter how many times I explained it. And then we'd end up having the same argument for the umpteenth time.

Bottom line, I was still married, even though Rodney and I were in the midst of an ugly divorce. To Maine, that meant I was a free agent. But to God (and me) it meant that I was still a wife. It didn't matter that Rodney had been having affair after affair since the day I married him (more precisely, since the day I started dating him).

My husband and the term "faithful" were like east and west, never the twain shall meet. Another reason why Maine was all, "girl you better snap that up before some hoochie comes along and shoplifts that bootie right from under you!" Yes, my best friend. The Poet.

Shaking myself into focus I grabbed my purse, my water bottle, and my phone. It was almost nine and Connie B. was adamant about babysitting hours.

Yes, we literally call my daughter Connie B. Her middle name is just the initial B., her godmother Maine's idea. Something I'd found cute, until Cardi B. and her musical stylings hit the scene. Then I wanted to take that B, turn it into a P or just kill it all together. Which was not happening since it seemed to make Connie B. a cool kid at her school overnight. More importantly, I loved it because Maine's grandmother was called Annie B. and she...is... AWESOME! Don't even get me started on her. I'll just say that she's the love of all our lives and leave it at that.

Hurrying toward the door with my head down trying to locate my car fob, I didn't see the brick wall I ran into coming. But I should have smelled it. Because, while my purse, my phone, and my keys were now gracing the Radio 100 studio floor, my water bottle and my face were buried in man-smell heaven. And, consequently, were wrapped in man-smell arms, all in an unnecessary attempt to steady me.

Fix it, Jesus! I groaned in my head.

"You alright?"

I wanted so badly to remove my face from the shaking wall of woman-nip but suddenly, I couldn't remember exactly why I should. I mean, it was obvious that he was laughing at me, so that was reason enough right? No. Not really.

"Uh, Naomi? While I appreciate the bear grip of a hug – how strong are you? I really like breathing so if you could just..."

"Oh!" I nearly shouted it as I jumped back, almost tripping (again) over my dang purse.

Fix it, Jesus, PLEASE!

"My bad. So sorry. I have to, um..." I couldn't even understand what I was saying I was so caught up in grabbing my stuff off the floor. I had to get out of there. Just recently, this man had become my kryptonite. Kryptonite I avoided at all costs. I'd made God a promise after Rodney, one I refused to break, even if said Kryptonite smelled like it could convince me to do otherwise. I barely heard him clearing his throat as he helped me pick up my stuff. But I heard it. And since I wasn't rude, I couldn't ignore it.

My head tilted to the side as I accepted my keys and phone from him, I waited. I didn't have to wait long.

"You know I always enjoy the podcasts, right? It's usually good, sound biblical teaching and advice all wrapped in a fun way, letting people know that it's okay to not be perfect and not try to fake it..."

Hidden in his pause between saying that and whatever was about to come next, I heard it loud and clear. A big BUT was coming, one I wasn't sure I wanted to know about. My instincts were sound as I was not wrong.

"But you do realize that your preoccupation with your sister's looks is a bit white-washed right? I never pegged you as somebody that was color struck you know? And hearing that tonight, you talking about your sister's soft hair and pretty eyes versus your natural hair and even prettier brown eyes? I... it was just unexpected, that's all."

It took everything in me not to rear back as if I was slapped. Because I'd never been accused of being white-washed (code for being brainwashed by the "white is more beautiful than black" propaganda that has polluted our country since the first black person stepped off the slave ship)

My mouth was gaping like a fish as I mentally cast about for a strong denial or sound reasoning contrary to what Vic said. Not that I was convinced that I was white-washed, mind you, I didn't feel like there was a white person alive more beautiful than me… just my sister. Only her. Which means that I couldn't possibly be whitewashed. But saying that was a lot harder at the moment.

"She ain't whitewashed! My girl knows she's all that. And you haven't ever heard her compare some white person to herself where she came up short. Facts are facts, that's all. She just pointed out the facts that every man thinks when she and her sister walk into the room together. Destiny is the first and the last thing they see. Period."

Thank God for Besties!

"Not me," Vic answered Maine before turning his head back in my direction, eyebrows raised, "I don't think that. When you walk into the room Naomi, I see you. That's the fact that I know."

Facing back toward Maine, he finished his one-man speech with, "And maybe you should take a poll. You know, ask the men in question before you go assuming you know what we believe and all. I have a feeling that you won't find your facts so factual if you did."

And he might as well have dropped a microphone, taking that as an opportunity to perform a textbook military one-eighty before trekking back toward the operator's booth.

Maine and I, mouths hanging open, stood there for a full minute before either one of us moved.

I was the first to break the silence.

"Did he just…"

"Yep."

"Did I just…"

"Yep."

"Should I…"

"Nope. It's ten minutes until nine. You got a sixteen-year-old that thinks she's your momma to get home to. So, get there. We'll hash this one out tomorrow."

"Right."

And that was exactly what I did. And I did it trying really hard not to remember that I heard what I thought I heard. Or that it made me feel all warm and fuzzy inside.

Chapter 3

"And where have you been? You do realize what time it is?"

What made this little scene so hilarious? Not the fact that my sixteen-year-old stood in the middle of my foyer tapping her foot at me. She had her arms crossed and frowned at me like I was the sixteen-year-old sneaking into my own house. Nope, what had me moments from collapsing in a hysteria of laughter was my three-year-old son that stood the exact same way as his big sister, had his arms crossed as well and wore the same exasperated frown on his face.

Right. Time to shut this foolishness down like, right now.

"So, what we are not going to do, is act like you were the one in labor with me for twenty-six hours..."

There it was. The teenage eye-roll. I mentally rubbed my hands in glee because I wasn't even remotely finished.

"Or act like I owe you any kind of explanations about my whereabouts when I was the one that stayed up late nights when you had fevers..."

"Really Mom?"

"...ear infections..."

"Okay M..."

"...the flu or a stomach virus..."

"Mama, I get it..."

"Oh, I don't think you do Boo, because last time I checked I'M the one that pays these here bills, puts the food in that there refrigerator and funds the totally unnecessary monthly expenses that begin and end with your cell phone bill, your various music subscriptions, and Netflix."

Blessed silence. And what made this moment even more hilarious? My three-year-old's head swiveling back and forth from me to my daughter during that entire conversation, like an eager spectator watching a tennis match. I guess the silence on my daughter's end (and possibly her head thrown back with her eyes closed tight in frustration) was all he needed to determine the winner.

I knew that to be the case when his little arms dropped and he launched himself at my legs, giving me my normal leg hug greeting with his normal, cursory, "Hey Mamas."

That's right. My son called me Mamas as in plural.

"Hey, son. You good?"

"I bressed."

I grinned. Because on occasion my son's normal, cursory greeting morphed into our family declaration. And when someone started on that course of action, it was the job of the entire family to chime in and finish it.

And right on cue, I and my two daughters (one of which from the depths of the house, probably her room) asked as one, "in the city?"

"Yes," he shouted with a little hop and clap. Man, I loved this kid.

Again, perfectly in sync, we asked, "And we're blessed in the field?"

"YES!" He shouted again, this time with two hops and two claps.

Trying hard not to laugh, I chimed in with my girls as we confessed the last line, "and we're blessed when we come in and go out?"

"Bressed! Bressed! Bressed! No longer able to hold it in, I let the chuckles escape as I swept my boy up into my arms.

I watched my eldest grin at my youngest before she remembered that she was supposed to be mad at me. And I knew when that happened because the grin disappeared, her eyes rolled (again) and then it came – the deep sigh of teen distress followed by the dreaded moan of despair. This nice little display of a teen being tortured was followed by a dramatically flung, "Lord, deliver me!" Before she flounced to her room where I heard the door close quietly in the distance.

The only thing missing from that scene? A hand thrown over her forehead, her head leaned back with her other hand flung strategically at her enraptured audience.

Only we weren't all that enraptured. My son and I turned from her recently vacated spot and looked at each other.

My eyebrows went up.

His shoulders went up in a shrug as if to say, "Don't ask me why you had crazy kids." Right before he flung his arms around my neck and gave me the loudest (and wettest) cheek-kiss a three-year-old could give.

And that's when the phone rang. I tried not to grimace. But it was hard not to since home was my sanctuary. That said, when I was there, phone calls became intrusive little gremlins that stole what little time I had to devote to my kids, away from me.

Of course, that line of thought has me grimacing as I pulled the time sucking menace of a device out of my pocket to see who dared interrupt my solace. Something that had my kids face all scrunched up to mimic mine (the reason I tried not to frown in the first place).

Bestie, the display read. Oy

Now, my head was thrown back dramatically (belatedly I'm seeing where my daughter gets this from) as I click on my touch screen to take the call. But before I could get out a single word...

"It's Annie B. She fell. She fell down the stairs, Naomi... and no one's here. I don't know how long she's been down here like this! I..."

Cutting off the panic I hear coming using my stern Mama-needs-you-to-focus voice, I half shouted, "Maine. Stop! Did you call 9-1-1?"

Tearfully, her voice raised another octave, "Two minutes ago. She's not responding, Naomi. What do I do? What..." the rest of the sentence cut off in a garble of incomprehensible words that did nothing to help the situation anyway, I cut her off again.

"I'm on my way. Go with the ambulance. Text me the hospital and I will meet you there. Do not panic! You hear me?"

"Oh my God, Naomi..."

"What I say?"

Sniff, "Don't panic."

I tried to smile reassuringly at my boy who was now looking at me like his world was ending and he had no idea why. Which was exactly how I felt.

"I'll meet you at the hospital. That said, you know you're not alone. Who's with you?

Another sniff, this one less pronounced, "God is."

"And if He be for us?"

A deep sigh with no sniff this time, "Who can be against us."

"Now get it together. She's gonna need your mind right when she wakes up. I'll see you soon."

Another sigh, "You get on my nerves."

I couldn't help but grin through the phone as I put down my boy to grab the keys I'd just dropped on the small table by my closet door in the foyer, "I know. It's why you love me."

A sad chuckle was all I heard before the line disconnected; something that didn't bother me one bit. We never said goodbye. Not over the phone, not when we were parting company, not at all. We left each other always with the expectation of seeing each other the next day. Annie B. had taught us that. I just hoped, as I yelled out where I was heading to my oldest, that in Annie B.'s case, that hope would be fulfilled.

***

I hated hospitals. Always have. I'm not sure if it was the smell; the sterilized bleach odor making a poor attempt to cover the stench of death or death itself. Whatever the case, since the day I sat in the emergency room at 9 years old after my sad attempt to climb a tree in competition with my cousin Freda, I've disliked hospitals, urgent cares and clinics with a deep, burning, seething hatred that hadn't abated over the years. At all.

Rodney had nearly lost his mind when, instead of going to a primary care physician during all three of my pregnancies, I'd seen a holistic nurse practitioner and midwife that saw patients out of her home. I'd told him it wasn't my fault he'd married a weirdo. Had I known then what I'd learned years later over the course of three extra-marital affairs, I would have told him he was lucky that fear of hospitals was my weird flaw instead of the need to seek vengeance over fidelity issues. Let's just say that I'd had quite a few Lorena Bobbitt thoughts over the years and leave it at that.

It was only my love for my bestie and Annie B. that had me gracing the halls of St. Luke's Hospital in Chesterfield, MO. A chill raced up my spine as I'd entered the emergency room doors and approached the nurse at the intake table an hour ago. Directed toward the waiting area instead of past the emergency doors, I'd texted Maine as soon as I sat down. And waited.

My phone buzzed with a text from my oldest, checking in for a status I couldn't give twenty minutes ago. Texts from the family came flowing in after that, with no response from Maine yet to the status check text of my own. Which is why I was probably shocked near speechless when Destiny, followed by Mike and her best friend Lindsay, came rushing into the waiting area.

Like I'd said during the podcast, I loved my sister. It's just, well...during times of crisis her presence hadn't proven to be an asset.

Case in point, the look on her face as she came rushing toward me told me everything that she said before she had a chance to say it. Her manner was panicked and frenzied and her wide, tear filled gaze practically screamed vulnerable. Ugh.

I didn't do vulnerable. Well, I could try, but times past have taught me what my entire family knows; not only did I not break into tears during crisis – EVER... but a sick part of my inner id saw problems as opportunities; challenges or mountains to be climbed and conquered. I was that girl that, if you told me I couldn't do something, I'd show you better than I could tell you that I could AND do it better than you.

So, when I'd tried to do "vulnerable" to manipulate my husband into honoring our wedding vows? He'd laughed and asked me if I ate something funny because the expression on my face was all sickly and pitiful.

Yeah, that happened. Therefore, I leave vulnerability to women like Destiny who could pull it off flawlessly and stick to what I know that's applicable; in this case, prayer.

"Oh my gosh, oh my GOSH Nahmi!"

And here we go. Okay, I won't expose my petty bone by pointing out that my sister is the only black female millennial that says, "oh my gosh," in the entire world; I won't. Making sure that my facial expression matched the concerned, yet welcoming sister look that I've practiced in the mirror several times, I opened my arms and waited for what came next.

True to tradition, my sister literally fell upon me, weeping in misery (not pretend by the way). Destiny was empathic by nature. Other people's pain and suffering magnified her own. She reminded me of Gus in the TV show Psych that always claimed to be a "sympathetic crier." If anyone broke into tears in close vicinity to where Gus was standing, he'd do the same.

All it took was a matter of moments for the front of my shirt to be completely drenched. It was with a mixture of relief and pain that I felt my sister hauled from me and into the arms of her best friend; the kid I'd never been fond of to begin with that reminded me of that fact as she ground her spiked heel into my right foot.

By the time Destiny was able to visually focus on me, the tears of pain in my eyes were very real. Teeth gritted in agony, I mentally asked God to forgive me for the tirade of pure cussage that I was about to let loose on Lindsay's blond, perky, barbie-like head, when I was cut off by a growling Maine who'd just entered the waiting area.

Wow. This growl was an entirely new sound. Wondering what the heck that was all about, I was in the process of asking just that, when my phone buzzed again. Seeing that it was Rodney, I let it go to voicemail, mentally reminded myself to call him later and again focused on Maine.

"...lucky I love me some Jesus or I would have let her have it with BOTH barrels! I specifically told the lady at the front desk that you would be coming and to direct you back to Annie B.'s room."

Arms crossed, hip out with the other leg stretched out told me better than words that this would not be the average tirade. If I didn't jump in and distract Maine soon, this entire hospital experience was going to go sideways from bad into possible jail time and community service: aka, worse.

"Hey! Maine! Did you see Destiny, Lindsay and Michael? They made it out to come check on you... and Annie B."

There were only a few signs that indicated to me I'd succeeded in my mission to distract and de-escalate. While Maine stood there, completely still in the same pose she'd adopted, her gaze didn't. Her eyes (with no movement of her head, mind you) had shifted to the left, taking in Lindsay and Destiny (both smiling creepily in their apparent attempt to be comforting) before shifting again to the far left where Mike stood, back propped to the wall with ankles and arms crossed. I hated the half smile and head tilt he sent my bestie's way. Mike had always been Maine's crush and he knew it, cultivated it even, with constant flirtation and little touches. But apparently, she was not his "type" when it came to dating.

However, since the smile served its purpose for now, to distract Maine, I pursed my lips to head off the sneer about to possess my face and rounded my eyes instead; instantly becoming the epitome of innocence (in my own mind at least).

My obviously fake round-eyed look became authentic in two seconds (only with surprise this time) as Vic and Tony prowled into the room. And child, do I mean "prowled". Have you ever seen a man walk into a room, his gaze assessing every corner of it before settling on you?

Well, I have. Three times in my whole thirty-four years of life. It happened once in high school after we took third place in the girls' basketball state competition my junior year. My high school crush, Jeff Jones (white guy – don't judge me – blonde headed with that old wrestler Rick Flair's appeal) had prowled into the gym to congratulate us.

After his round of cursory hugs with the cheerleaders (all white by the way) his blazing blues had settled on me, followed by a grin that possessed all the charm of Justin Timberlake, Jesse McCartney and Brad Pitt. I grinned back, figuring it was my turn for a cursory hug from the most popular (white) boy in school. Only the hug was anything but cursory.

A sister got squeezed? Squz? Sqozen? Whatever the correct term, that hug had been long, tight and definitely repentance worthy. By the time he'd let me go every single one of those cheerleaders had been glaring daggers at me. And I had been so okay with that.

The second time I'd witnessed the prowl had been when Rodney had made his grand entrance into our statistics class at Webster University. Tall, chocolate and full of swag, several women of various ethnicities had sucked in their breaths as he stepped into the classroom. And while I hadn't audibly sucked in air like so many did around me, my hormones had made note of this new threat to my focus along with the rest of my body, which ignored my mind's blaring alarms and flashing warning signs. I'd gotten more than a hug from Rodney; the only thing good out of all he'd put me through? Our three beautiful children.

And then there was this time, right now, as Vic entered the waiting area. When his gaze finally landed on me, my hormones and body went through the same protocol as it had with Rodney, only this time, it listened to my brain's reminder to be cautious.

So, when he finally reached me, I did NOT inhale deeply to catch that scent of him that I so loved. Instead, I pasted on my, "See, I'm a good person... really... "smile and croaked my, "Hey Vic," greeting while gazing slightly over his right shoulder instead of into his warm chocolatey eyes and braced. Because the hug was coming. And unlike Jeff Jones' hug, I longed for this one with every fiber of my being. And Vic being Vic? His hug did NOT disappoint.

Chapter 4

My apple watch flashed the time at me. It was just past 1:30 a.m.

I was exhausted. I don't quite remember taking my clothes off, showering or putting on my pajamas, but I couldn't help but remember the events of that day. They kept repeating in my head; an endless loop of fear and confusion.

So now, laying under my covers with my arms behind my head I stared blindly at my ceiling. After two hours of waiting and probably breaking nearly every bone in Vic's hand as I did so, we finally received a call down from Maine. She let us know that Annie B. had regained consciousness and, beyond a fractured hip and concussion, appeared to be okay.

Relieved, I'd briefly hugged Destiny, then Vic before packing up my phone, charger and note pad. My mind shifted to the next task: to get Destiny then myself home. After just thirty minutes of waiting, both Mike and Lindsay had apparently decided that they weren't willing to invest another second for more info on Annie B.'s condition; so, Mike had decided to head home and drop Lindsay along the way. I'd agreed to take Destiny home since she'd wanted to stick it out.

Vic had been adamant about following us; first to Destiny's and then to my place. I did NOT argue with that. I couldn't even remember a time when Rodney was more concerned about my safety than he was at making it to his next Blerd (Black Nerd – and yes, it's a thing) group meeting or some work event. And, while I'd been sure Vic saw me as a sister or a close cousin (we'd grown up with him and my grandparents that lived on the same street), there was a part of me that wished he wanted to keep me safe for other reasons.

That's the thing though, I refused to lie to myself – an agreement I'd made with me, myself and I when I'd gotten that lesson from Annie B. in middle school. Of course, my parents, my teachers and all the rest of the civilized world taught me that lying at all was bad. Out of all of those, it was Annie B's suggestion that I'd taken most to heart.

"Folks lie babies. That's the world that we live in. Men lie so they don't hurt your feelings. Women lie so they don't hurt a man's pride. Kids lie because they don't want their butt beat. In all that, remember this. Whatever lies you find yourself telling for whatever reason, never – EVER – lie to yourself. If you can't trust your own mind, who will you trust?"

So, I accepted it; my kinship with a man I – a still very married woman despite the separation and current divorce proceedings, was deeply and viscerally attracted to.

Which was also why I'd gaped at him for an embarrassing full minute in shock on my front porch after he'd followed me home.

Anyone that knows me knows that I am a "matter of fact" individual. The old folks call that a "straight shooter". I call things as I see them, and I don't pull punches or dance around facts to preserve feelings. It's a waste of time and frankly, irritating as all get out when someone does it to me instead of just getting to the point.

Thus, when I'd thanked Vic with a quick hug and grin before turning to unlock the door and he'd grabbed hold of my hand to pull me back to him, I'd jerked in surprise and froze up in confusion as his arms wrapped around me again.

"You know everything is gonna be okay right?"

Closing my eyes, I sank into that hug like I was right where I needed to be. Seeing no need to mess up the moment with my doubt and anxiety, I nodded, adjusting my arms to close around him and held tight.

My head resting on his heartbeat, I allowed myself to drift on that sensation of peace and safety, just for a moment. I was so lost in it that I almost missed his softened voice rumbling so close to my ear that his warm breath sent tingles up my spine.

"And you know that, no matter what happens with the divorce, with Annie B… with anything, that I will always be here for you, right?"

"Mmmhmmm." That was all I had to give him as I snuggled even closer into his warm hold. I did this despite the warnings blaring in my head to stop, get my fast tail into the house and close the door. Feelings of peace and safety shattered, giving way to a hint of something else. A something else that I needed to escape before I ruined our friendship by doing something stupid; like using his butt as a hand hold.

"And you know that, when it's all said and done and the divorce is final, it's my turn to shoot my shot, right?"

"Mmmmhmmm," I mumbled again before my brain screamed at me to focus on what was just said.

Wait, what??? Blinking rapidly, it felt like it took forever for my head to shift from comfortably resting on his chest (where the staccato beat had increased in tempo along with his breathing) to lean back where my gaze was arrested by his very hot one.

My body understood the implication long before my mind did. My mind was asking unnecessary and irrelevant questions like, when did we start talking basketball? And, I wonder how accurate his jump shot is as I hadn't seen it since we were kids.

All that was going through my head while my heart was about to beat itself out of my chest. Every single part of my body that made me a woman stood up to take notice. This was something I should have anticipated because I'd not had "relations" since leaving Rodney over a year ago.

My very baffled expression appeared to be lost on him before his hot gaze turned contemplative, his eyes narrowing followed by that signature head tilt. I could see his mind working as his stare lingered, first on my eyes, then my mouth. Apparently, taking in my obvious shock (my eyes were so huge in my face that my eyebrows were probably touching my hairline and my jaw that ached from how wide my mouth had fallen open) Vic hesitated.

His hold loosened but he didn't let go. His head straightening from the tilt and I felt the deep breath he took before his eyes grew hooded.

"Naomi, you have got to be kidding me."

I didn't respond. I didn't have to. My mouth had gone from hanging open to working soundlessly, searching for the words my brain scrambled to find.

"I know that games aren't your thing, so, while I'm reconciling myself to the fact that you are NOT playing around, a part of me refuses to accept that you are really that oblivious."

My teeth clattered as my jaw slammed shut. Then my arms dropped before repositioning against Vic's chest and exerting the pressure I needed to loosen his hold further and take a step back. There are apparently knee-jerk reactions that women possess, triggered by various situations; like if their children are in danger; or in this case, when a man calls them "oblivious."

My inner dialogue ranged from, "Oh no he did NOT just call me oblivious," to "is he for real?" My attitude however, settled somewhere between the two as I felt that person I called "old Naomi" start to rise.

"I'm sure, Mr. Carter, that your intention wasn't to call me oblivious; however, that's exactly what you just did. What behooves me is that, with no clue provided before tonight about you wanting to 'shoot your shot' as it were, I'd like to know how one could possibly assess my unawareness as obliviousness?"

Like magic, right before my eyes the crinkly lines around Vic's eyes disappeared and reappeared around his mouth, his full lips stretching out into a very masculine grin. I completely ignored the goosebumps that were popping up all over me at such a wondrous sight and instead, folded my arms across my chest in mock exasperation. I say mock because it was just that. When a man smiled at you like that and made the hair all over your body stand on end, exasperation wasn't the ruling emotion.

"You're mad," the grinning mouth filled with perfect, beautiful teeth said.

"Why would you say that?" I huffed, crossing my arms tighter.

"You got all educated on me." His grin widened.

51

"What?" I grouched.

"Whenever you get nervous, mad or tipsy, your words get all precise and contain three or more syllables."

I attempted to go all "Maine" on him by raising one eyebrow. In my head, that happened. In reality, both eyebrows were probably touching my hairline. Which is why (I'm sure) that his head went back on his shoulders as the chuckles slipped out, almost as if they came out against his will.

I was really starting to hate how cute he was, especially when he smiled. I ought to punch him in his cute, smug nose and see how funny he thinks that is.

Instead I did what I did best... I deflected.

"Did Maine say when they would be releasing Annie B.? I need to let Big Mama know. You know how close those two are. Do you think it's too late to call her and let her know? But if I call her then I have to call everybody else which means I'm gonna be on the phone until Jesus comes back. Maybe I should..."

"Hold on, hold on; HOLD ON WOMAN."

My lips went from flapping to inward, clutched by my teeth to prevent my own chuckles from coming out against my will. This was an old trick of mine. I've found that one thing that all men tend to have in common is that they are problem solvers. Throw a bunch of life situation equations at them at once and not only are they distracted; they are completely discombobulated. Linear thinkers that most of them are, I've noticed that they need to approach things one at a time, preferably sequentially and in order from most urgent to the least. I've seen it done to the point where a man would just turn around and walk away, right in the middle of the discussion. Not that I was hoping Vic would walk away, mind you. He's pretty. And he still smelled good. So, you know... I was just going for shutting him up.

A giggle slipped out at that thought despite my effort to hold it in.

Which is probably why the wrinkles left the edges of his mouth and reappeared around his eyes. I knew that he'd figured me out and I was about to get it. It was sad that a part of me purred in a 1960's Marilyn Monroe voice, *bring it*.

And I was about to say just that when my phone buzzed. I'd had it on silent while at the hospital.

Checking the screen, my eyeroll and deep sigh all but shouted at Vic who was on my phone. And seeing that I'd sent him to voicemail twice earlier that night, I figured I'd better answer before I had to hurt the man.

"Yes, Mr. Carmichael?

"Where are you?"

I felt my own eyes narrow and wrinkle before glancing up at Vic's expression noting that he was doing the same. That's probably because he could hear Rodney loud and clear seeing as how he was dang near yelling in my ear.

"Why is that your concern, exactly?

"Because I need to know why the mother of my children has left them alone while she corralled around with some bald-headed dude until 11 p.m. at night."

Oh no he did NOT. My mental female dog meter had just entered the phase def-con II. It was the stage that preceded somebody getting cussed the heck out. And by the look on Vic's face (it had gone all tight and you could tell that he was clenching his teeth), I was going to probably have to fight him for the honor. I took a deep breath to get my temper under control. And opened my mouth to respond when...

"Are you there? Are you still standing outside with some random negro while my kids are in the house by themselves?"

And I was gone because, really?

"First of all, how do you know where I'm standing and giving me a physical description of Vic who you KNOW?"

There was a breath and a pause before, "It's Vic?"

"Yes, its Vic. He followed me home from the HOSPITAL where Annie B. is after having a bad fall with no one home; something that isn't your business, but I felt like showing you how stupid you sound right now. What I need to know however, IS your business; that business being

HOW do you know that I'm standing outside, on my porch, talking to ANYONE, let alone what time I arrived home?"

I was so mad that I was literally seeing red. Either the creep was having me followed, was watching me himself or was tracking and recording me somehow. Any of those reasons of why he knew what he did was absolutely insane and ridiculous; something I shouldn't really be surprised about since those two words tended to describe Rodney perfectly.

Rodney, as was his way, hymned and hawed for two minutes, probably trying to give himself enough time to make up a good lie. A lie I didn't have time for. And I was about to say exactly that when,

"I know she just did NOT raise her voice at you! Who does she think she's talking to like that?"

"Mia!" Rodney interrupted. But it was too late. Because, despite being in the background (apparently Rodney had me on speaker) I heard all of that. And since I was already mad, I was ready to give her a taste of me.

I tried to remember who I was. That I was blood bought, born again, and not the same petty, bitter and angry person I used to be. Sadly, my mantra to "keep old Naomi in a box" failed me. I knew this because I heard the following trip from my lips:

"Oh, the homewrecker speaks? How interesting. Should I use small words to express how I don't care about what she thinks… AT ALL. Or do you need to translate that to her in sign language?"

I watched Vic's eyes round and then squint as he bit his lips. Yeah brother, you just saw how low the real Naomi can go, I thought. I tried to reel in that ugly side of me, but it was too late. Old Naomi was out, and she was ready to draw blood.

"Did she just…" Ugh. I hated screechers. So, I shut that nonsense down with,

"SHE is right here Ms. Thang. So, you can direct anything you have to say to me, TO ME. And Rodney knows where I live. Just march your little hot thighs on over here so I can insult you better in person. And then, if you're still feeling froggy? Jump."

I heard two more screeches before I heard the click. Rodney's hanging up ended that by-play with such finality that I had to swallow my next threat. That's when I noticed Vic was bent over at the waist.

Was he laughing at me? He was! He was actually laughing at me. Which was awesome if I were trying to be funny. But I wasn't, so what was up with that?

I didn't have the opportunity to ask that question because Vic, still laughing mind you, had wrapped me up in another hug before kissing my forehead, then leaning his forward so that his forehead was touching mine.

The incredulity at his humor in a non-humorous situation had fled to be replaced by something so warm and glowy, I forgot about Rodney, that girl and everything else. I even forgot about the awkwardness I'd felt when Vic explained how he planned to "shoot his shot."

That moment of complete secluded bliss was the first I'd experienced in a long time and I wanted to stay there forever.

But we couldn't. Vic's hands had gently held my face in place as he kissed my forehead again before advising me to get some rest and that we'd talk more later.

A statement that made me so uneasy, instead of getting the rest he'd suggested, I was wide awake at one thirty in the morning.

Was I ready for another relationship so soon after ending things with Rodney? Granted, we'd been separated for about a year, but still. Emotionally, mentally and in every way except physically, Rodney was still my husband. A husband that I was never good enough for since he couldn't stop stepping out on me. A husband that had always been critical; one I constantly had to change myself for to please; efforts that didn't work or make our marriage stronger.

And what about Vic? We grew up together. We played in the creek behind Big Mama's house together. We hunted frogs on family trips to what we called "the country" (my families land up in Carlyle, Illinois) together. I'd always thought of him as a friend until now. One of the sexiest, best smelling male friends I'd ever had, it's true... but still a friend. What, exactly, would happen to that friendship if things didn't work out between us?

It was that last fear that decided what my mind knew I should choose. I wasn't ready. I wasn't ready for another relationship. I definitely wasn't ready or willing to risk what Vic and I had built together as friends on our possibly being a compatible couple.

On that note, I had to get to sleep. I had work in the morning. Sweet sleep; that's what God's word said He gives to his kids. Remembering that, I surrendered my fears to Him and made my decision. I was better off single. Vic and I were better off as friends.

Sleep hit me then like a Mack truck. Which was great until I woke up the next morning realizing an uncomfortable truth. I'd dreamed about Vic and what it would be like to be his all night long. Was it any wonder that I longed to go right back to bed?

Chapter   5

Vic...

"Yo."

"Did you tell her yet?"

"Bye Tony."

Vic would have grinned if he could. Tony had bugged him about putting his feelings for Naomi out there. Feelings that he'd had for Naomi for as long as he could remember. She'd been his first crush, his first kiss (she was only 6 when it happened but he counted it) and the only woman that he could imagine himself starting a family with.

Pulling into his driveway, he jumped out of his Dodge Ram and headed toward his back door, completely distracted about what had gone down that night.

Because how could she not have a clue about how he'd felt about her? How he'd always felt about her? But then, he should have known that it was a possibility. He'd figured that she'd known in high school despite their doing everything as a group of friends. Vic, Maine, Naomi and a few others had all gone to homecoming and prom together. No dates, just friends hanging out. But it was always Naomi that he put his arm around protectively when they were out and about. It had always been Naomi that rode in the front seat of his car when he drove the group to events, parties or the neighborhood hangouts. Vic hadn't made his move back then because he'd been determined to make his mark on the world first.

And though he'd been drafted by the Arizona Cardinal's football team after choosing to enter the draft his sophomore year at Purdue, he'd assumed that Naomi would finish her degree at Webster and be at home in the Lou; waiting for him after he'd made a name for himself in the NFL.

Instead he came home after finishing his first season to find her married to some dude she'd met in one of her classes. And pregnant.

What was a brother to do but assume that it wasn't God's will and move on?

But Vic hadn't moved on. He'd tried to though. The thing is, it was hard to move forward in life with a different woman when every woman you dated came up short in comparison to the one that got away. Either the woman wasn't tall enough, or friendly enough. Maybe she didn't smile right; the kind of smile that made a brother stop short and try to catch his breath while he enjoyed the view.

Thus, while Vic had gone out with those women, simulating a life that he didn't have in him to live; he'd bided his time. Because while he didn't dislike Rodney (much), he'd known from the first day they'd met that something was wrong with that brother. Known it deep in that place inside that something didn't add up.

Vic blamed his distraction for what happened next. Reaching to unlock the back door, he jumped back in surprise as the door was ripped from his hand and pulled inward. It was annoying, his brother Azariah (AJ for short) standing there bent forward cackling at his reaction. Lowering his left arm that was pulled back, ready to deliver the punch of a lifetime to defend his life and his home, Vic pushed forward through the door, knocking his brother on his butt in the process.

"Very funny, chump." Vic groused, dropping his keys on the counter and moving to his right to turn on the kitchen light.

"Aww. Did I scare the big bad retired football player?"

Opening the refrigerator, Vic was tempted to turn around and tackle AJ like he'd done several times when they were kids, but he liked his kitchen the way it was. Instead he retaliated in the way that had brought his mom peace in her latter years; verbally.

"And which one of us is sprawled out on the floor after being knocked on his butt? Not me, bruh."

Snorting, AJ stood and dusted himself off before pulling out the kitchen chair to his left and flopping down on it.

Vic frowned, hearing the creak but too hungry to address his brother's carelessness.

"Fix me one, too... please?

Vic half turned at his waist, his mouth hanging open. AJ was the baby of the bunch. Born a preemie, he was just six months younger than Vic. Abnormally small as a child, both Vic and their other brother, Xerxes (or Zee as they called him) had been overprotective of AJ in the extreme. Something that led to him being what the rest of the family called "spoiled". But, as lovable and goofy as he was, Vic and Zee had never regretted keeping their brother close and safe. Except for at times like this. All grown up and with a place of his own, AJ managed adulting fairly well except for when it came to cooking or cleaning his house.

Which was why he'd probably used Vic's spare key to enter his house and squat in his kitchen. He was waiting for his brother to come home (for who knows how long) just for Vic to fix his grown butt a sandwich.

Vic smacked his mouth shut, shook his head and focused on finishing what he'd started. While brooding. He tried not to do that, brood that is. But when it came to Naomi, it had become a lifelong pastime. So, it was with distraction and out of habit really, that he made two pastrami, ham and turkey subs, cut them in half, placed them on plates and dropped them onto the kitchen table, one in front of where he intended to sit, the other before his brother.

"Oh, and can you hand me..."

"Get your own water man, I am NOT your maid," Vic grunted.

"Well, you don't have to get an attitude about it," AJ grumbled, hopping up from the table, his sandwich already half gone from the three bites he'd taken in less than forty-five seconds. It was something that had always amazed Vic. AJ had been born weighing just shy of three pounds, a far cry from his currently standing a foot taller than Vic at six feet six inches and weighing in at over three hundred pounds. The growth spurt of all growth spurts hit him at thirteen and hadn't stopped until he was nineteen. Vic grimaced, remembering the many shattered dishes, broken furniture, bumps and bruises that had resulted during AJ's adjusting to his new size. The entire family had lived in terror that they would end up homeless, he'd been so clumsy.

"Talk to Zee?"

Vic paused in chewing on his second bite, realizing that he hadn't. Which was unusual. He and his brothers were extremely close. For many reasons, their father being the main one. Zee had been the oldest, the most responsible and reliable of the three. Appointing himself man of the house, Zee had always looked out for the family. He'd been a better father and role model than their dad had been.

"Nope, why? What's up?" Vic had waited until he was done chewing to speak up, a courtesy he didn't expect from AJ, something he was right not to do since AJ didn't hesitate to respond, mouth half full of the rest of his masticated sandwich.

"Just haven't heard from him and thought it odd. Especially when he said he'd be getting in touch with you this week."

"Why," Vic asked, then took another bite.

AJ shrugged, smacking his lips and grinning before he answered.

"He heard Naomi was getting a divorce."

Vic frowned, chewing. When AJ didn't elaborate but instead, sat there grinning like he did when he snuck and got high in the ninth grade, Vic grunted.

"Okay. And?"

"And what?" More grinning.

Dropping the rest of his sandwich, Vic half stood, reached over and slammed his left fist into AJ's right arm like he did when they were kids playing the frog game.

"Hey! Come on man! You tripping!"

Vic ignored AJ's pout and his obviously failing attempt to rub away the burn from his arm.

"And what, punk?"

"Mama told you not to call me that!"

"Well, Ma isn't here anymore is she?" Vic grimaced. It was out before he could catch himself. Hearing AJ's quick inhale and pained groan, he knew that there was no amount of backpedaling that could fix it either.

"Man, wait…"

AJ had jumped up, dropped his dirty plate into the sink and was at the door before Vic could get it out.

"Nope. Not waiting. I'm up."

"AJ..."

"I'm up, man! Obviously, you've got a bug up your butt and I ain't Zee. I can't talk you through it to help you figure it out. Not gonna even try, especially when you determined to piss me off. Thanks for the sandwich."

Vic watched his brother slam out his back door, growing more irritated. He wasn't irritated with AJ or even Naomi. He was irritated at himself.

Because he had done something he hadn't done in years; taken his anger and frustration out on his brothers. It had been two years since they'd lost their mom, but AJ felt that loss more keenly than he or Xerxes – which was saying something since Vic still felt as if something had exploded and, to this day, festered in his gut. And because Vic and Zee had always been big on protecting AJ, they'd been careful the last two years when it came to talking about their mom. Vic and Zee had learned to cope with the loss. But for AJ, it was like she'd just died yesterday.

No longer hungry, Vic dropped the other half of his sandwich into the trash. Dumping the remnants from AJ's plate into the trash as well, Vic placed the dirty plates into the dishwasher and mentally added talking to Zee to his to do list for tomorrow at their monthly meeting.

After the accident that cost him his football career, Vic finished his degree in Information Technology at Purdue. Not really something he wanted to do, still and all, it was his back up career path and just about all he knew. Always the entrepreneur, Zee had talked him into partnering with him to open a small IT solutions firm that handled cyber-security and managed corporate technology infrastructures. Not seeing many options out there with a pay scale comparable to the salary he'd drawn in the NFL, Vic had jumped at the opportunity. And he hadn't regretted his decision. In less than 5 years' time he'd gone from part owner, part employee (hardware set up and tech support), to managing those departments, to a partner that only came in once a month for managerial reporting and staffing updates. It wasn't until recently that he and his brother decided to take on other entrepreneurial opportunities.

Vic cringed as he headed up the steps to get ready for bed. He hated the "talks". Deplored them actually – every... single... one. The "parental talks," aka his usual talks with Zee when it came to his personal life, the "relationship talks," with the women he'd dated but could never really commit to. It was those talks that were the worst. Vic couldn't remember how many times he'd nearly just gotten up and walked out on several of those sit downs. They were usually a complete waste of time, tend to end up stating the obvious and always resulted in his frustration.

But he wasn't one to shy away from what needed to be done. And this talk needed to happen. Because he'd just wounded his little brother in the worst way, something he normally would never do.

"God, I need you to help me out, here. I want your will. I really do. But I'm not gone lie... I want mine too."

It was that prayer that Vic went to sleep with that night, on his lips; his heart and his mind. He had no idea that God's will aligned with his in the best way. So, that wasn't really the question weighing on Vic's slumbering heart. It was the question that had remained consistent through the years when it came to Naomi. Was he willing to pay the cost that his goal would entail? Because it was going to cost him, of that Vic was sure. And though Naomi was well worth it, Vic wasn't sure that he could pay the price; no matter how badly he wanted to.

Naomi
The next day,
Big Mama's House...

"All I want to know is why you didn't call me? We would have hopped in the car with some bats and chains and rolled out on a brother! That's how we roll fam!"

I groaned, dropping my forehead to the table as it seemed (at least to me) that the entire Brooks clan gathered around me and Big Mama who were both seated at the table.

Cousin Fred, the one speaking, was standing there waving one hand wildly in the air and snapping while his other hand rested on his bright-orange skinny-jean clad hip. Flamboyantly gay and fitting every diva stereotype in the book, Fred was a Brooks; which meant one thing: if you come for one of us, you came for all of us. And all of us could and WOULD retaliate in kind.

I watched Big Mama hide her grin behind a huge mug filled with coffee, pretending to take a sip instead of laughing like she was. I could tell she was laughing because her way-too-thin shoulders were shaking slightly. Why couldn't my family be normal? Why couldn't they just talk about the man like a dog like everyone else then go on about their day? Oh no, that would be too easy. Instead, we have to go out like a Scottish clan at war with another, rolling out with bats and chains.

Why Lord? Why?

"But really? Fred is right and you know it! You really should have called me immediately! I'm your attorney for crying out loud! He's obviously having you followed Naomi. Most likely by a private detective. He wants to dig up dirt on you because he's planning something!"

And that was cousin Freda or "Free" as we call her, Fred's less than feminine but very conservative twin. One of the few voting republicans that did not (and still does not) support Trump, my beautiful but tomboyish cousin was almost the mirror opposite of her twin brother.

"Freda..." I started but knew I wouldn't be allowed to finish. Because Freda had said all that she had to say on the subject. In fact, from the look on her face I could tell that she was already working out strategies to offset any pitfalls or traps that Rodney was attempting to set for me. And sure enough, my less than favorite and what we like to call "ghetto" cousin Elaine, added her two cents.

"Alright! That's what I'm saying. Where this negro at? I got me some new steel toes and a brand-new stun gun in my car. Naomi and I will take him, Fred and Michelle got the chick. Make sure y'all kick her teeth in. Make that heifer have to suck out a straw the rest of her life!"

Big Mama choked on her coffee at that. Good. Because I was tired of her laughing at this craziness. Where was her sage wisdom and calm control that normally cooled these heated situations? I opened my mouth to ask only to be interrupted by Michelle.

"I don't want the chick. Let me at that punk. I'll kick him in his Petey Wheatstraw, knock him on his tail and Naomi can stomp his face in."

My mouth dropped open. Because Michelle, only nineteen, was my baby cousin, the last born of our generation of cousins. She was sweet, soft spoken and effeminate in every way. A born seamstress with a promising future in fashion design, my baby cousin was the go-to for baby-sitting and clothes making throughout the family. Except for today, apparently. Who was she trying to be? The Gucci gangsta?

Big Mama choked again on her coffee, a sign that I'd unintentionally said that last part out loud. I did that sometimes. So, when my forehead hit the table this time, it was to several laughing voices echoing off the kitchen walls.

An unspoken prayer was answered for peace when Destiny glided in with her chipper and bright, "Hey Family!"

And, as usual, all attention shifted to her, to Michael and how the plans for their June wedding was coming along. For the first time, in a long time, I was extremely grateful for my little sister garnering all the attention in the room. But my family, as crazy as they were, had only just begun with their shenanigans.

Please God, give me a new family... one with some common sense, I prayed desperately in my head.

In my heart and mind, I could hear Him chuckle His, *"Why would I do that? And if I did, how would you fit in?"*

I groaned again; my head still planted on the tabletop. Because as always, He was exactly right.

Chapter 6

"Alright friends, families, hater's and hater-cators – that refers to those of you like me that are inclined to educate haters the world over..."

"From sea to shining sea!"

"Maine!"

"What?"

"This is not the national anthem, dawg."

"So."

"So? Ugh. May I finish?"

"May you finish... what?"

"My intro into today's podcast!"

"No, no... I mean... may you finish... what?"

"Do not stress me female. I will chop you in the throat."

"Big Mama taught you better manners than that. And I bet she's listening right now..."

"Please! May I finish please!"

"Yes, you may."

"You irk."

"So does your mother."

"Charmaine Marie!"

"Fine. I take it back. Sorry Mama Beck, you don't irk nearly as much as your daughter does."

"She's not even listening tonight. Can I continue now?"

"By all means."

Thunk.

"That, dear listeners, was the sound of my best friend's head hitting the table for the what? Twentieth time this week?"

I groaned. Because Charmaine was in rare form tonight, it had been a crazy week and, from what I could tell, it wasn't going to get any better.

The downturn of the week started with Annie B.'s scheduled hip surgery. Charmaine had been unbearable and half-crazy when the doctors confirmed Tuesday that surgery would be necessary. While it wouldn't be an entire hip replacement; due to Annie B.'s age, there could still be complications.

Before her fall, I would have never deigned to call Annie B. frail. That opinion changed Tuesday afternoon on our visit. She'd seemed so much smaller than normal. While she wasn't ever a big woman, her personality and spirit always filled a room. And when she and Big Mama got together? Whoo! Those two filled a room with such love and power, it was a tangible thing; an energy that sparked and energized every person that breached its perimeter. Observing Annie B's shrunken form surrounded by the white linen of her bed covering and pillows brought home like nothing else did how fragile life truly is.

My week didn't get better from there. Because my family's threats against Rodney were NOT an idle thing. Thus, I've had to keep tabs on all of them to make sure they didn't do something stupid. By stupid I mean something that would affect our divorce litigation adversely. Oh, and because it would have been wrong. But you know... more because I didn't want to lose. I'd given that man too many years of my life for him to get away with one iota of the foolishness that caused our marriage to end.

Keeping tabs on my family meant checking in at random times; one of which I'd caught Elaine just as she was waltzing into the car dealership where Rodney worked. A sitch that would have ended so badly that I would've had to move out of the country to avoid the backlash. Lucky for me, I had dirt on her from last year. Juicy dirt too. Dirt so juicy that, should her common law husband, Andrew, find out, she'd have to let him watch ESPN football all year with no interruptions; literally hell for her.

It also meant that, after receiving two or three pics from Michelle's cell phone of Rodney at the entrance of Ray's Barber Shop and Tony's Doughnuts, I'd had to call and threaten her to withhold visits from her favorite baby cousin (my son) if she didn't quit it and take her butt to class.

And last, keeping tabs meant that I had to schedule and attend an impromptu appointment with my attorney... who was still mad at me, by the way. Which meant that I had to hear her fuss... and fuss... and frikken fuss during the entire consultation. At the end of said meeting, I was ready to skewer my ears out with a hot poker. Sadly, most people don't have fireplaces, as such; there were no pokers just laying around.

I wish that had been all. Working for the State of Missouri's Children's Division full time was a draining, thankless job that never ever ended. Kind of like parenting. Only, the rewards and happy times were much farther and fewer between than those one enjoys when raising their own family.

Case in point, one of my families that had been scheduled for a routine check in today. The history with mom, a former drug user that had been so high she'd laid her 4-month-old on a hot plate; was so riddled with abuse, a vicious cycle of her own mother's addictions, that every visit and conversation with her broke my heart. She sincerely wanted to change and give her kids better. But as the word says, the spirit is willing; but the flesh is weak. It was the same weak flesh that I battled when I denied the urge to text Rodney about my day or ask him how he was. I understood her pain. My battle was far different; but Rodney was once my drug of choice – just like meth had been hers. Both were no good for us. Both would kill us if we'd let them, emotionally or physically. And yet, even knowing that, there was that part of us that hungered for just a taste every day.

Then, there was Destiny's phone call. She'd checked in to get Annie B.'s status... and because big mouth Fred had called her and told her about Rodney having me followed. It hadn't been mentioned since I'd been all but forgotten about at the house. That said, even when you think you've gotten away with something free and clear, good ole' Fred made sure that didn't happen. Which irked me to no end.

Because my little sister was... how can I put this? She reminds me of an anime character. One whose eyes get all big and round with innocence and wonder. It was that kind of innocence that drowned her in disbelief when the people of the world acted like asshats. It was also the kind of innocence that wants to hug or feed away your troubles (now I'm not gonna lie, a sister would NOT have turned down IHOP had someone offered) not understanding that the injury runs so deep, nothing but the love of God could touch it.

So, when she'd offered all of this on my behalf as she has done for as long as I could remember when life hit me in the gut, I always loved... and hated... her a little bit more. It was such a strange dichotomy that when Charmaine once joked that Destiny was someone she loved to hate; I'd told her she had it backwards – my sister was someone you hated to love. But you couldn't really help it – she was just that great a person.

And last, there was Vic. Just remembering this week had me raising my head from the table to stare off into the booth where he and

Tony made magic for us. Watching his beautiful, bald head bent in concentration over the controls was something I was finding I could do all day. It was like, he'd always been attractive; always been a good guy, good looking and really good smelling. But once I'd found out that he wanted to be more than friends? His attraction factor quintupled.

The parts of me that had gone dormant (after realizing that my husband had been sharing what was mine far and wide, despite our counseling due to his former infidelities) woke up with a vengeance. My body buzzed with awareness as I struggled to control my breathing. Which was, just my luck, right when his gaze snapped up to meet mine, like he felt me watching him. My breath caught in my chest then. And my gaze dropped to his mouth as I watched him lick his lips.

Oh boy oh boy oh boy. Everything in me felt like it was on fire. So, when my gaze found his again, the half grin he threw at me before his stare fell to *my* lips (lips that I was subconsciously licking) set me near to combusting.

"HEY! Ms. Thang!!! Can you stop with making the sex-eyes at Vic in the control booth and finish what you were about to say?"

How God? How could you have possibly thought it a good idea to make HER my best friend.

There had to be murder in my eyes as my narrowed gaze flew to meet Charmaine's amused one; I say that because I was imagining her in a blonde wig as Maria Antoinette. And I was her executioner, in complete control of the guillotine that was about to chop her head off. It was a visual I very much enjoyed as I ignored Tony's snickers in my headset before proceeding with my introduction. It was either that or actually kill her.

"As I was saying before I was rudely interrupted..."

"And staring at Vic." Maine giggled.

"I. Will. Cut. You."

"Sorry." Snicker

"We were talking about hater-cators such as me and my FORMER best friend here and promised to get into what we have affectionately coined THE HATER'S PRAYER."

"And to those of you that left the snide comments last week but didn't share the podcast on facebook or insta... you suck."

"Thank you, Maine."

"You're welcome Nahmi. Do continue."

"Ehem. The Hater's Prayer... let's get into it. First though, we ought to explain that there are two types of haters..."

"Just. Two."

"Exactly. The first kind is the kind of hater that you want to be. "

"The pimpest hater there is!"

"That too. And while Maine likes to call it having a pimp mindset, something the comedian Katt Williams describes as, I think pimp, therefore I am pimp – I tend to refer to it as being mentally tough."

"Well, the brain IS a muscle."

"No, it isn't"

"Yes it is, google it."

"It's an organ Maine."

"No it's NO-OOOTTT."

"I hate it when you sing your disagreements."

"Too ba-aadddd."

"Anyway, the mentally tough hater. You my friend, are the hater that uses admiration to fuel your inspiration."

"And to change apathy into determination."

"Stop rhyming. I thought we agreed that we are not Dr. Suess?"

"As a cure for your frustration."

"Maine!"

"To be like the Father of creation."

"OR, there is the hater that is ruled by envy. An envy that leads to one of the seven 'abominations' listed in God's word. Also known as a person that causes division between friends and family."

"This is the type of hater you want to avoid."

"Exactly Maine. And if you find yourself being one of those haters?"

"Kill yourself?"

"Charmaine!"

"Just kidding."

***

"This one was really good."

I blinked at Vic as he walked around the table, collecting headphones and wiring. I wanted to say something witty or fun. Or sexy.

But all I did was sit there and blink at him.

Because the fact remained that I wasn't ready. The fact also remained that, despite not being ready for a new relationship, I still wanted him like a hungry puma wanted a wildebeest. Desperately.

I was so busy trying to stop my voracious blinking while simultaneously searching for something witty and flippant to say, that I failed to notice Vic's coming up behind me. This was possibly why when his hands landed on my shoulders from behind, I jumped so hard that the top of my head hit him smack under his jaw.

The snap of teeth followed by the grunt of pain made me want to crawl under the table or magically disappear to a land far far away. Sadly, I couldn't do either as my body wouldn't move. The best I could do was tilt my head back and say a heart-felt "I'm sorry."

"You going to kiss it to make it better?"

I swallowed. Because no. I was not going to be kissing anything to make it better or anything else. Which was why I swallowed again.

Vic had lowered until his mouth hovered just over mine, Spider-man style. If he licked his lips again it was over. I was done for. And half of me longed to be totally done for.

"So, best friend. Before we head out, we need to talk merch and a streaming opportunity that just fell into my lap."

I was surprised that Vic didn't jump from Charmaine's interruption. Still hovering right above me, his head turned until his focus rested on Charmaine standing in the door. My gaze helplessly followed. And I had to fight not to fall out laughing. The sly grin on my best friend's face was obviously sending Vic the "back off" message.

I sighed in relief as Vic straightened, looked back down at me and winked, before walking out.

"Girl, you are so in trouble." Charmaine grunted as she pulled out her chair and flopped into it.

"I know right? Thanks for the assist."

"Anytime. Though, I don't get it. You like him, you're attracted. He likes you and always has. He's still attracted. Why do I have to play road blocker again?"

"I'm not ready." I mumbled, rubbing my eyes to clear my suddenly tired vision.

Maine snorted. "You looked more than ready an hour ago."

I chuckled and Maine joined in. The truth was, if this thing was just about the physical attraction, I'd have been making the walk of shame three days ago. But it wasn't. I was still married. And I didn't bother to point that out. To Charmaine, once Rodney had cheated on me, any allegiance I owed to our marriage was no longer an obligation. And since I'd explained that numerous times before only to get the same, "Whatever!", I changed the subject.

"You mentioned something about merchandise and streaming just now?"

"Oh! Sorry, I got sidetracked. Yeah, I have this friend who works for Purefix. It's like, Netflix for Christians. Anywho, Dennis, my friend, has been listening to the podcast for a while. He said he loves it so much that he's gotten his entire family listening in and watching our video's on YouTube. He asked me a few days ago if I thought you'd be interested in taking this show to a streaming platform that can be featured on Purefix."

"You're kidding, right?"

"Really? Because that's the kind of thing that I would joke about?

Before she could finish her sentence, I'd hopped up, jumped over to her chair and bear hugged her up out of the thing. My squeal was so high that every dog in a ten-yard radius was probably collapsing in pain at that moment. Before I realized it, Charmaine and I were both hopping and squealing, squealing and hopping, all the way to the radio room door.

Barely noticing an astonished Vic and shocked Tony we hopped and squealed ourselves all the way to the elevator, down the three floors to the exit and to our cars.

A welcome, refreshing change in our lives from the worry and strain of worrying about Annie B., divorces and being followed, I relished the moment of sharing such a promising idea to a future with endless possibilities.

Which was probably why I realized upon arriving home that, I still hadn't sat Vic down to let him know that I needed time. And I really needed to do that. I was task avoiding. I wanted him. But I also wanted the comfortability and calm nurturing peace that had come with my marriage to Rodney. With Rodney life had been consistent, comfortable and... well, comfortable. It was exactly what I'd always figured marriage should be like. It was what Big Mama and Grandpa Joe had when he was still alive. It was, if anything, what I would have expected a relationship with Vic and I to be like.

I was coming to find out that I couldn't be more wrong. Because instead of just inciting the normal feelings of security and peace that Vic had always inspired in me growing up, I was feeling heat. Not just heat, but THE heat. I'd never felt this way about any man, any crush; not even any of the book boyfriends I'd had over the years (the leading men in romance novels that I liked to read). Which was exactly why I needed to get on letting him know that things couldn't go any further.

I knew that Vic would understand if I told him as soon as possible. But he would view any procrastination on my part as a denial of my feelings and desire for him. It would be justification enough for him to keep trying.

And that would be a very bad thing. Not as bad as one's ex having them followed around by a private investigator. But close enough.

Chapter 7

It was 3:30 am. That explained why my brain couldn't assist me with connecting the dots for everything that was happening now.

Connie B. was shaking me, shouting, "Ma, your phone!" My cell phone was going off like a fire alarm and my bedroom lights were blaring into my eyes, making it very hard to focus. So, when the ringing stopped and started again, this time playing the music from the *Dream Girls* movie soundtrack (Destiny's ringtone) I finally put two and two together.

I realized that I was not in a mineshaft, trying to dig my way through a cave wall to my children on the other side to the sound of Rodney's evil laughter. That had been a dream. All right, I told myself. You're okay. The kids are okay, it was just a dream.

My heart rate slowed enough to where I could breathe and focus on the next part of this paradox of merged realities. Connie B. was answering, then handing me the phone I hadn't been lucid enough to answer myself.

"Ma. Ma! Wake up! Its Lindsay! Something happened to Aunt Dessie!"

Well, that did it. Lucidity crashed into me with such force, I was jolted upward and, before I realized it, diving for the phone. The look on Connie B.'s face broke my heart. It didn't take a genius to realize that a three in the morning phone call from a person your mother couldn't stand, was urgent to the fifth power.

"What's wrong?" I nearly shouted into the phone.

The background music was too loud for me to hear clearly. Because of the static laden connection, I could only decipher two words out of what Lindsay was saying, "Destiny...static... static... shot... static...out."

Which was pretty much all I needed to hear to catapult me out of the bed and into clothes while tossing my phone to Connie B. with instructions.

"Pull up the locate app that the family logs into and get Destiny's location. Text it to Maine and tell her to meet me there. Tell her to call Fred on the way."

Connie B., ever the efficient teen that she was when it came to technology, completed my requests in half the time that it would have taken me to and, before I knew it, I was dressed with my phone on speaker, flying out the door and jumping into my car.

I didn't have to worry about who would be there to help because by the time I got there, Fred would have had the whole crew in his old jeep Cherokee and on the way. Like I said, I was a Brooks. And when we rolled out, we rolled out deep, prepared for anything.

"Let me punch her in the face. Just once. One time. I promise."

I held tight to Maine's arm to keep her solidly by my side. Because I knew she wasn't joking, not even a little bit. And I felt her pain.

In front of me stood a half sober Lindsay, giggling in the face of me, Charmaine and my cousins. She was giggling in (what I hoped) drunk, fascinated horror at what she'd caused.

So, here we stood, being bumped and jostled by a crowd of bourgeois young professionals at Club Ice, a new joint in the Central West End.

Known for its unique business model of operating a networking studio during the day, Ice opened its doors every Friday at 6 pm for a 24-hour stint of non-stop partying before shutting down promptly at 6 pm on Saturday to ready itself for the coming week. The club was membership based and nonmembers could only attend by express invite from a high-ranking member. Destiny was one of those. And though she knew this wasn't my scene, she'd left Charmaine and my names as anytime guests with the bouncers up front. Bouncers that refused to let my cousins in. Bouncers that were taken down by the twins in a matter of minutes, allowing us to pass through. Something that had to be completely emasculating since both stood well over 6 feet and were effectively neutralized by a girl and a gay.

Charmaine's raised eyebrow at me promised us a good laugh in the future over that one, but right now we had to focus.

Locating Destiny had been our primary concern. We hadn't wondered why we heard no sirens or saw any police cars, though we probably should have.

Instead, we'd made a beeline toward the bar in the center of the room before I caught sight of the platinum haired head just below the waving arm.

Beside said head and arm was the prone form of my little sister strewn across a table, while the other hand of the platinum headed arm waiver rubbed her back.

By the time we'd intimidated the crowd enough to open completely for us to make our way to Lindsay's side, I was so angry I was vibrating. Because it was clear that, while unconscious for some reason, my sister was not bleeding out from a gunshot wound, nor would she be anytime soon.

So as soon as I'd gotten within ear shot, the words, "I'd better see a bloody gunshot wound somewhere on my sister or you can cancel Christmas," leapt out of my mouth.

Watching Lindsay's eyes round in seeming shock before she burst into giggles had me divided where my reactions were concerned. There was the calm, logical Naomi that quickly explained that things aren't always what they seemed and that it was a bad connection so I should hear Lindsay out as she quickly outlined the events of the night that had led to this moment.

And then there was the other Naomi. The ice cold one that wondered how many punches I could land before the cops got there. She was the Naomi that Charmaine read like a book which led to her willingness to take my place with a more self-controlled solution of delivering only one punch. I loved it that my best friend was willing to take this hit (or in this case, deliver this hit) for me. But the smart Naomi, the one that understood consequences, won out over the two. Thus, she was the one that spoke next.

"What happened?"

Both of Charmaine's eyebrows went up as her head went backward on her neck as if she'd been slapped. Right before her eyes narrowed and breath huffed out of her nose. And of course, I read all her non-verbals as if she'd spoken out, loud and clear, "REALLY? That's it? So, we are just going to ignore the fact that she is laughing right now? No. Just. NO."

Instead of responding with nonverbals of my own I gave her the words, "Hold on Maine, gunshot or no, Destiny never gets drunk and never passes out in public. We need the facts and Lindsay has them. Okay?"

My best friend grunted. I could read her desire to punch something and wasn't far behind her as far as that desire went, so I turned to Lindsay this time and gave her my lifted eyebrows, not trusting myself with more words because of her incessant giggling.

"Girl!" Fred shouted, "Quit doing your bit as a hyena from the Lion King and TALK!"

Maine grunted. So did Freda right behind me, who was tapping her foot. This was about to go sideways in the worst way. Lindsay had guffawed at Fred's comment, something that led me to believe she wasn't all that sober. And since Elaine was still focused on the crowd and music instead of the conversation, I figured I had 2.5 seconds to get Lindsay together before all hell broke loose.

Snapping in her face like I used to do when they were in middle school I shouted, "Hey! Get yourself together and tell me what happened to my sister before I hurt your feelings in all the worst ways that I know you hate."

The giggles stopped almost immediately, her smile replaced by a wrinkled forehead and narrowed gaze filled with spite. Since she'd been Destiny's best friend almost as long as Charmaine had been mine, I knew exactly which buttons to push. Adult or no, I wasn't ashamed to pull out all of the stops despite how many sour memories that would bring up for Lindsay; times when Charmaine and I had embarrassed her or Destiny or both on numerous occasions to keep them from following behind us to parties and school events. But I didn't have time to be sensitive to her feelings. Wait no, that's not right. I may have had the time, but I didn't care enough about her feelings to even pretend like I did. What mattered was my sister, getting answers and getting them now.

"I…" Lindsay started, before pausing, her head tilting to the side as if she were trying to remember.

"You what?" I growled. Because Elaine was now paying full attention which meant all of the ghetto in the room was about to congeal upon us like bacon grease getting cold.

"I left her at the bar with these two guys to dance with their friend. They seemed cool enough so I figured she would be okay."

I breathed deep. I had to keep calm. If I lit up like I wanted to then Elaine wouldn't be far behind which meant a police presence would be required for sure.

Charmaine elbowed me and nodded to my left. One glance in that direction showed that the bouncers had recovered and were heading our way with reinforcements. We were almost out of time.

"How long were you gone?" I rushed.

"Uh…"

"Spit it out kid!"

"Don't call me kid… not a kid anymore you know." Lindsay slurred.

The bouncers were just ten feet away.

"Got this," Maine commented in a low tone that wouldn't alert Elaine before moving.

And as if on some unspoken cue, Elaine stepped up, her switchblade appearing out of nowhere in her left hand.

"Need me to cut it out of her Cuz?"

"Elaine.."

"Forget that. This heifer left Dessie with some punks. Punks she didn't know. She got a lesson coming, and I just clocked in to teach it."

"What you gonna do Ghetto Queen. You gonna do something? Well do something!"

I knew right then that Lindsay was flat out drunk. She wasn't tipsy or just buzzed, she was gone. Because she knew Elaine. She knew my family. We were not the ones to make idle threats. If Elaine said she would cut her, she meant exactly that. It was a truth that had me jumping in front of my cousin and grabbing hold to her right wrist that had already flipped the blade in and another out, ready to start "teaching her lesson".

"Bouncers to our left. Maine can't handle that by herself! She needs you."

My soul breathed a sigh of relief as Elaine glanced to my left and her right. Her eyes got big before lighting up with humor, something that caused me to slowly turn to my left in fear of what I was about to see.

And that's when I deep breathed again, this time with a bigger sigh of relief as what I saw affirmed that God really and truly loved me more than I realized.

***

Vic

The 911 text Vic got from Charmaine had him jumping out of bed, throwing a tee shirt on he'd grabbed out of a drawer to go with the basketball shorts he'd donned to sleep in. He'd grabbed his Jordon's laying by the door, slipped them on and raced to his car, keys, wallet and cell in hand.

Club Ice was only ten minutes away from his place, but it was ten minutes that felt like forever as he pulled into the restricted parking area where his pass allowed him to park. Urgency riding his back like he was a rodeo bull, Vic burst into the front doors noting the absence of Murphy and Rockwell, the bouncers on rotation with growing fear.

Propelled inside by that escalating terror, Vic's gaze was drawn immediately to the two bouncers in the crowd, one with Charmaine on his back yelling in his ear, the other sinking as he watched, the area between his shoulder and neck a victim of what looked like the Vulcan neck pinch by Freda Brooks.

Watching as three other employees approached the scene ready to intervene, Vic moved fast. His football training, always a part of him, came in handy as he weaved, moved and pushed, navigating his way seamlessly through the crowd to get there before the other employees could grab hold of Charmaine.

Snatching her off the bouncers back, Vic stepped in front of her moving quicker than the eye could detect as he caught the punch swinging in Maine's direction in his hand.

Pushing the punch away as if it were a child playing at fighting, Vic reached over to his right to snatch Freda behind him as the other bouncer collapsed.

Recognition dawned upon the bouncers and employees and gave them pause. A pause that was long enough to kill the altercation altogether as Vic nodded his head toward the back of the room where the executive offices were located.

As the employees and bouncers obeyed and, as one, trudged toward the back of the room, Vic, with Charmaine and Freda grasped by the arm on each side, approached what looked like a relieved Naomi.

Catching sight of the switchblade in Elaine's hand, he couldn't help but shake his head in full understanding. Elaine was apparently in a cutting mood, something that never boded well for any of them when they were growing up; a state of affairs that hadn't changed all that much.

Depositing the two at Naomi's side, Vic kept it brief.

"Be back in a minute. Find out what happened."

With that, he headed to the back room to do what he did best. Fix people's messes.

Chapter 8

Naomi

I haven't had to undress my sister since she was in middle school and had her tonsils removed. That said, I was a tad uncomfortable undressing my unconscious sister's form to put her in the night gown that Connie B. had supplied. I settled for removing her shoes, pulling the blanket over her and making sure she rested on her side before turning off the light of my guest room and closing the door.

I found Vic (who'd carried her from my car, up my stairs and into the guest room where he'd laid her down for me) standing in my kitchen near the back door, his back resting on the wall with his arms crossed, head down and eyes closed.

I took just a moment to look my fill, a dangerous undertaking considering what looking at him tended to do to me. Especially when I'd decided that, despite what looking at him did to me, that him and me were not a good idea. Too bad my libido didn't agree as my psyche played tango music with me vibrating to the tune of it.

My breath caught when his eyes opened and his sizzling gaze immediately met my own, catching me in full stare. Desperate to break the moment as his little flirty half smile appeared, I blurted, "So, you were gonna tell me why those bouncers asked how high when you told them to jump?"

The grin widened.

"No, I wasn't actually."

"Excuse me?"

"Baby... I really wasn't. Because you were going to tell me what happened tonight?"

Okay. So, the baby thing just threw me completely off when it came to witty or flirty rapport. My body responded with a vengeance, however. Mentally grappling my hormones into submission, I turned my focus toward what had happened to my sister.

And felt the anger inflame me all over again. And I was beyond angry, passed livid, and well into straight up enraged. Because not only had my beautiful, innocent baby sister been drugged, a recording of her in a back room being pawed by two men had surfaced on Instagram... a recording that was going viral as we speak.

As I remembered finding out exactly what had happened from a few girls that had stepped forward (and not Lindsay who had been off cavorting with some unknown guy) I recounted to Vic every detail.

While I talked, I noticed the slightly flirtatious smile slide away to be replaced by a frown that was growing more thunderous by the moment. I was almost hesitant to finish with the statement that disturbed me the most but, to me, had to be spoken.

"And when I say we blew Mike's phone up by calling him nonstop, I mean we blew it up. I wouldn't be surprised if that thing is sitting somewhere in a billion pieces at this point, we called him so much."

"With no answer or response at all?" Vic asked this with his lips so thin I barely saw his teeth as he spoke.

"None whatsoever."

The only physical response that hinted at what Vic was feeling was the fisting of his hands under his arms.

Something that caused a sense of peace to flood me. Because this was the Vic that I knew; protective, supportive and a great listener, Vic had always been our champion if we needed one. And I was so relieved that this aspect of Vic hadn't changed that it wasn't even funny. The truth is, this new-fangled passion and heat between us had me discombobulated in the worst way; especially since I knew that it was time to make sure he knew where I stood regarding that.

"So, you gonna tell me why the bouncers listened to you or what?" I hedged, task avoiding the conversation that I knew we should have had yesterday.

"My brother and I are... we have ties to the club."

"What kind of ties?"

"The kind that, when I speak, people listen."

It was my turn to speak through the thinned lips. I hated feeling like I had to pull answers from someone like a dentist going after an infected wisdom tooth.

"And that kind would be what exactly?"

Vic shrugged and looked toward the door. I could tell that the current conversation was making him uncomfortable, but I didn't care. It was either him be uncomfortable with this line of communication or me be uncomfortable with the other one.

"Mommy?"

My eyes narrowed as Vic visibly relaxed against the wall before turning to watch my three-year-old toddle through the kitchen door, rubbing sleep from his eyes. Suspicious, I searched for the other child that wouldn't be too far behind only to catch a quick glimpse of a scarved head disappearing behind the wall to the left of the open kitchen door frame.

Deep sighing for what I hoped would be the last time that morning, I grabbed hold of my baby boy as he reached me and hugged him tight.

No longer looking Vic's way, I didn't have to hear the words, "saved by the toddler," to know that's what he was thinking. Unfortunately, he was correct in that assumption. When my babies entered the scene, it was all about them, and anyone that knew me knew that.

"Hey baby boy. And girl," I said that last part loudly to let my middle child know that she'd been spotted and to come out of hiding, something she did while directing a shy smile Vic's way before planting herself along my left side so I could hug her close as well.

Vic grinned her way as he came away from the wall with a steadiness that sealed the finality of our conversation.

"Call you later?" He asked with a head up chin raise my way.

"Yep," I responded as I watched him turn and head toward the back door that led to the garage where we'd parked to bring Destiny in.

"Pancakes Mamas." My boy said with such bossy finality I couldn't help but roll my eyes. Because it was Saturday morning and pancakes was what we did.

Instead of responding that it was too early or that his mom desperately needed sleep, I kissed his forehead before staring into the beautiful browns of his big sister at my side and asking, "Pancakes baby?"

Her exuberant nod sealed the deal as I set about doing my favorite thing in the world besides fantasizing about kissing Vic... loving on my kids Bobby Flay style.

But that other part of me still remembered that things were about to get real in the worst way for my little sister. And I had the worst feeling that I would be catching some of that real too; something that I was NOT looking forward to.

***

Outside of Mike's Condo
That same night...

She was watching him again, something he was always oblivious too. It was easy to tell that he was watching the video. Observing his reaction as his mouth fell open, she smiled.

It was an evil smile she knew, but then, she was completely alone so that really didn't matter did it? The glee that she felt at watching his face turn three shades of red almost drowned her.

She'd been waiting so long to see this. Ever since that day, the day she'd found out that they were dating seriously, she'd known that this was going to be necessary.

You couldn't help who you loved right? And her love was almost a physical thing – a physical thing that soured and curdled like spoiled milk whenever they entered a room together.

It had taken months and months of meticulous planning... a plan that she'd hoped she wouldn't have to put into place, refusing to believe that this thing between them could possibly be serious.

Not only did Mike and Destiny have nothing in common, anyone that knew Mike could tell that he was just going through the motions... faking everything he could from his supposed tender emotions to his proprietary way of holding her close whenever they entered a room.

But she knew. She had known from the outset. And it was unacceptable. Because love couldn't be feigned or faked and before she was done, everyone would understand just how powerful and true her love was.

Naomi

I held the door open as Connie B. carried inside a tray laden with a cup of coffee, a glass of water and a bottle of Aleve.

Flipping the light switch I winced with guilt as my sister groaned before rolling over to pull the blanket over her head.

Thanking Connie B. in a whisper for her help as she lay the tray on the unoccupied portion of the bed, I waved her out and closed the door behind her.

Another groan sounded, muffled this time from under the blanket and I winced again.

I'd only ever been hung over once in my life. That first night with Rodney. That's right, I'd gotten mind numbing drunk on the night I lost my virginity to my ex. Subconsciously I understood a truth that I refused to admit to myself, that I'd made a huge mistake.

While that hangover experience had been so long ago, I barely remembered it, empathy for my sister and what she was going through along with what I was about to tell her gripped me.

Because not only had things gone from bad to worse, they'd been set ablaze by the fires of hell. And I had to be the bearer of all these bad tidings, something I did not look forward to.

"How are you feeling kid?" I whisper-talked, shaking my head as a louder but still muffled groan sounded in response.

"Come on sis. You need to get these meds and this coffee in you. We need to talk."

"Bttt whttt."

I wanted to want to laugh, but the situation my sister was finding herself in was so dire, I couldn't muster the humor that I normally would have felt at her almost indecipherable words.

"About last night and the crap that has hit the fan since."

The blanket came down with a whoosh. I watched as my sister turned a disturbing shade of gray at her rapid movement. I watched in sympathy as I saw her wrestle the nausea down with more strength than I would've had.

"Need the trash can?"

Her negative head shake was enough to convince me not to grab it just in case. That was one thing I knew about my sister; the trait that she shared with me and dad. She was extremely stubborn about being in control of herself. That's why we both did well athletically. Self-control and discipline were key factors in performing well consistently and we were all about performing well. Which was also why I knew that, once I told her all the hell that had broken loose, she was going to lose her mind.

I watched as she won her battle against the urge to purge with pride. As her eyes blinked open and she grabbed hold of the two Aleve I held out and the glass of water to swallow and quickly chase them down, I waited patiently.

Her eyes closed as she focused on swallowing, then clenched as her chest jolted. I watched her again wrestle down her body's instinct to rid itself of toxins the old-fashioned way and held the cup of black coffee (with a hint of peppermint extract in it) out to her when she was ready.

While she sipped, I slipped another pillow behind her so that she was better supported. Her sigh of relief as she leaned back to give her abs a rest was noted. I held my peace, however. She would tell me when she was ready.

And she did exactly that.

"Okay, I'm ready."

I smiled sadly because, no, she really wasn't.

I decided to come in with a soft approach first.

"What do you remember from last night."

She took another sip, her eyes closed. Her eyes moved under her eyelids letting me know that she was working on remembering as much as she could.

So, when they were opened, I wasn't surprised to find her gaze blank and puzzled.

"I don't actually... remember anything I mean. I remember Lindsay and I leaving for the club. I remember going in and I remember settling in at the bar. After that, everything is one big blur."

I nodded as she talked. Then braced myself for dispensing the information that I know would devastate her.

"Okay. Well, what you probably don't remember is the two guys that you met at the bar. Two guys that we've got the cops looking for now since we believe that you've been drugged. Charmaine took a sample of blood that Elaine drew to the lab to be analyzed for rohypnol. We also had a sample taken for Dr. Samuel, his exchange said that he would deliver the message that we would be bringing that in today for him to send off."

"Wait. I thought Elaine was fired from being a Nurse's aide last year?"

"She was, but she still carries some of the materials from former clients in her trunk. We were lucky she did, otherwise we would have had to call an ambulance. Things were already bad enough."

"Bad enough how," she asked warily, taking another sip.

I knew that the smile on my face held all the sadness that I felt at what I was about to say. But it had to be said.

"Not only were you drugged kiddo, you were... mauled in a back room of the club. A mauling that was caught on video."

"Oh God."

Her groan of despair hit me hard in my chest. Because I wasn't done.

"I couldn't reach Mike last night to let him know what happened."

At that her eyes flew open, "Where's my phone? I need to call him!"

I grabbed hold of her hands that were feeling along the bed as she looked at the nightstand hoping to catch sight of her phone. I knew I wouldn't have her attention any other way as I readied myself to say it plain.

"There's no need. He knows. He's seen the video. When he called, I tried to explain that you were drugged but he didn't want to listen. Honey..."

"What? WHAT???"

Her words were frantic. And broke my heart.

"He doesn't want you to call him, Destiny. He said he doesn't want to talk to you and... and that you're done. The weddings off."

Tears welled. And I wanted to scream. I wanted to scream as loud as I could and punch something. A feeling of helplessness overwhelmed me as the tears spilled over, quiet grief overwhelming my baby sister's beautiful face. In that moment, I hated everyone and everything. Because this was pain at its worst, and I could do nothing to shield or protect her from it.

Wetness fell onto our clasped hands as I held on tight. Because, at least to me, that wasn't even the worst of it all.

"And your boss at the St. Louis National News called. He said he needs you to call him as soon as possible."

It was with that last bit of horrible news that I pulled her shaking form into my arms and held on tight. She'd been drugged. She'd been mauled and publicly humiliated, a humiliation that was being viewed by thousands as we sat there. And then the one person in the world that should have been there by her side to shield her and support her at the same time had rejected her. On top of all of that, she may have just lost her job, a job that she loved beyond belief.

Holding her, I grabbed her ringing cell from my sweater pocket and dismissed the eighth call from Lindsay that day. She was a sucky friend as far as I was concerned and didn't deserve my sister. Nor did Mike.

And those were the words I uttered as I rocked her back and forth wishing to God, I had some way, any way to fix this.

Feeling arms close around me from behind, I raised my own wet eyes to meet the wet blue one's of my stepmom, the only person in the world that I trusted more than myself to take care of Destiny now.

Letting go, I slid off the bed as she took my place, rocking her child, shushing her in a way that I remember her doing when we were small and had hurt ourselves (or was hurt emotionally by someone else) in some way.

Closing the door behind me, I grabbed hold of Connie B. and Madison, both crying and hugged them to myself. And prayed to God that, as a mother, I never had to witness my babies being broken by the careless and evil handling of others.

Chapter 9

Vic

Pulling into his parking space behind World-Wind Technologies, Vic smiled. The inspiration for that name had been all Zee. "We're going to take the world by storm man, like a tornado or a whirlwind!" Ever the entrepreneur and skilled at wordplay, Vic wasn't surprised when his brother combined "world" and "whirl wind" to form "World-Wind" as their business moniker.

It was part of the reason why Vic considered Zee the brightest of the brothers. Zee was not only the quickest when it came to wit and charm, he was also the most dependable and responsible of the three. Zee took being the oldest brother seriously; a fact that Vic sometimes found to be a pain. But because Zee loved way more than he criticized, it wasn't too difficult to put up with.

Pushing into the lobby, Vic greeted Christine, the receptionist, with his usual nonchalant grin. Always careful with the employees to ensure his intentions weren't misconstrued per the regular cautious rant from Zee, Vic didn't linger. Instead he waved his hello at a few shouts acknowledging his visit and sped by.

Entering his brother's office to find him staring out the huge picture window that overlooked the Westport Plaza parking area, Vic dropped into the sofa across from his brother's desk, making himself comfortable.

Christine had most likely called ahead to tell Zee he was on his way up. Stifling a yawn at his brother's bland eggshell décor, Vic settled in. He wasn't in any rush to hear his brother fuss. But he knew he had it coming, nonetheless. And Zee being Zee, he didn't disappoint.

"So now we have date rape drugs being dispensed in our networking center?"

Vic's head hit the back of the couch. Because dang it to hell, his brother took being well informed to a whole other level.

"I'm handling it."

The half turn at his waist as Zee looked his way with no expression on his face caused trepidation to trip up Vic's spine.

Blinking with wide (and hopefully) innocent eyes, Vic returned his stare.

"Hmmm," was all Zee said before he turned again to contemplate the view.

But Vic knew his brother well enough to know he wasn't done. While Zee searched for the diplomatic response to whatever he had found out since they last talked, Vic took a moment to admire his brother's style.

The three brothers had always had their own unique look. Zee, being the more metrosexual of the three, was always dressed to the nines in either three-piece suits or slacks, a shirt and tie with coordinating Stacy Adams.

Today he'd gone for the black silk button down with the matching tie, slacks and black (some other famous brand) dress shoes. While the brothers were all bald, that was where their similarities ended.

Zee was the shorter of the three but was no slouch at 6'2". Athletically sound and fit, he bore a trimmer build than Vic's more musclebound form and Azariah's more bear-like quality. Zee glanced down at his own track pants and Jordans with a grin. Because he and AJ had always shunned the high-end look that Zee modeled, instead embracing their own; Vic's being more athletic while AJ's bent more toward lumberjack (as in jeans and plaid shirts).

"So, "Zee stretched out the word, breaking through Vic's distraction, "Our goal to remain anonymous, silent partners of the networking centers we hoped to sponsor in other cities... is that still a thing? I'm asking because you might as well have shouted our connection to Club Ice with your actions last night. I just wanted to know if you planned to do the same with the other three locations we're contemplating opening next year?"

Vic snorted. Guilt and sarcasm no longer worked on him when it came to Zee. That being the case, he didn't bother to acknowledge that statement with a response, allowing himself instead, to focus on the problem at hand.

"I contacted the Northside Police Department this morning. I wanted to know what we needed to do to prosecute these guys since they were dumb enough to record what they did."

Zee's back stiffened.

"They recorded themselves giving her the drug too?"

Vic cleared his throat, "Uh, no. No. Just touching on Destiny while she was passed out."

Zee sighed.

"And this thing with you and Naomi? Is that about to kick off finally?"

Vic felt his back stiffen. "What thing?"

Zee turned fully this time to face him, his hands now in his pants pockets.

"She's about to be divorced. You've been waiting on this forever. So, what are your plans?"

"Didn't we talk about this last week?"

"No, last week you told me I needed to mind my own effing business."

Vic grunted. Because as far as he was concerned, that was them talking about it. And to show his brother better than he could tell him that he'd meant what he said, Vic got up and walked out, closing the door on his brother's chuckles sounding behind him.

Naomi

"Go home girl. What are you here for anyway? Don't you and Maine have y'alls program tonight?"

I grinned as Big Mama rolled her eyes at Annie B.'s grouching. The coughing on the other side of the curtain brought on another snarl from Annie B., causing Big Mama to chuckle and roll her eyes some more.

The hospital had long since moved Annie B. from the critical wing into a shared room on the fourth floor, a state of affairs Annie B. wasn't all that happy about.

"I'm too dang old for a room-mate," she'd groused after calling her insurance company every snide name she could think of. With over seven decades experience of snide name calling, she could think of a whole lot, so that went on for a while.

The new room was smaller than the old one despite having two beds verses the one. And while Annie B. had the big bay window on her side, the bathroom and shower were on the other side of the pulled curtain. For this reason, Annie B's part of the room included a potty chair next to the bed. She also had a tv (hanging from the corner of the ceiling catty-corner from the bed), two chairs, her bay window, a nightstand, phone and her curtain.

It was cramped sure, but, as a family, we'd been cramped into much smaller places. That said, cramped was never okay with kids, thus Connie B. took pity on her siblings by walking them around, hoping to cheer them up. Between seeing their Aunt Dessie in her current state and hearing Annie B. fuss in such a small space, a change of scenery was very much needed.

Two days. That's how long Destiny had marinated in depression. Two long days of no talking, no eating, no anything. Even Lindsay had gotten frustrated and slammed out of the house when Destiny refused to respond. And that girl loved my sister like frogs loved flies, so you know it had to be bad. And, for the first time I didn't know in how long, I was at a total loss for what to do. Words of comfort refused to come. And anytime I found myself trying to encourage or bring my sister out of her funk, I'd just end up crying right along beside her. Nonstop. Something had to give.

Which brought back to mind why I was here. Not only was I having a very real, personal crisis due to my soon to be ex-husband's most recent round of foolishness, I was also mentally fatigued regarding Destiny's situation or the fact that Vic had taken what once was a solid friendship to a whole other level whether I was willing to go along or not.

And since I was sitting in a room with over 60 years of collective adult life experiences, now was as good a time as any to avail myself of their wisdom. And despite Annie B's bad mood, I figured it was best to ask my questions now rather than later.

"So, Destiny's depressed. She hasn't eaten, showered or left my guest room for two days."

"Now, that explains why you're here," Annie B. grumbled.

Ignoring Big Mama's shoulders shaking, I continued.

"I don't know how to cheer her up."

Big Mama snorted. "You don't."

"Ma'am?" I could feel the lines on my forehead deepen as I tried to understand Big Mama's simple answer. It was Annie B., however, that expounded.

"What, you think if you offer her ice cream for dinner, she gone all of a sudden, feel better?"

I shrugged. I hadn't expected exactly that. But something close.

"That girl got sucker punched by life coming at her from three different directions at once. Give her time baby. Hell, even Christ Jesus needed time when John the Baptist was beheaded. Two days isn't a lot of time."

I nodded, rolling my own eyes this time at Big Mama's shaking shoulders. And took a deep breath to ready myself to deliver the next blow.

I cleared my throat and swallowed.

Annie B's eyes narrowed, her gaze hitting mine with the precision of a laser beam. I sensed Big Mama's mood turn serious. I could feel the room grow tense and, while what I had to say next wasn't all that bad, it felt like both women were preparing themselves for some really bad news. And the longer I hesitated, the worse that feeling would get for them. So, I forced myself to just spit it out without preamble.

"Vic almost kissed me and told me that he wanted us to be together after the divorce is final." I said it so fast that all of it came out as one word. I breathed to get some oxygen and prepared myself to say it slower or at least explain further that revelation.

Annie B. grunted.

"Bout time," was Big Mama's answering growl.

"Ma'am?" I found myself repeating because, *What the Waffle*?

"Girl," again Annie B. expounded, "that boy been in love with you since the first day ya'll met."

"Annie B., I was all of six years old! And Vic was eight."

"Yes, you were," Big Mama interjected, "remember how you came running into my kitchen? You were livid. That new boy, you said, that new boy Big Mama — he just pulled my ponytail and punched me in the stomach. If he touches me again, I'm gonna kick him in his ding-ding just like Daddy told me to do to boys that put their hands on me!"

I grinned hard. Because while I didn't remember saying any such thing, it definitely sounded like something I would have said when I was six. In fact, I'm surprised that I didn't kick him in his ding-ding that first time. Big Mama

115

must have read my mind as she went on to explain.

"I laughed and told you that it's how boys say they like you and want to be your friend. I almost got you to change your mind but a scream from outdoors grabbed our attention. You remember that?"

"No ma'am, " I chuckled. "What happened?"

"Well," Annie B. interrupted to explain, chuckling herself, "your cousin Freda apparently witnessed said altercation and decided to introduce young Victavious to the family right and proper."

Big Mama laughed, her eyes glazed as she was obviously remembering, "We walked outside to a dogpile of your cousins on the boy. His older brother was there holding one of his legs trying to drag him from under them all while young AJ stood there screaming and crying for them to get off his brother."

I couldn't help but laugh right along at the picture these two painted.

"Us grown folks had to intervene to get them off the boy," Big Mama continued, "and, while young Vic would give you a contemplative look from time to time, he never put his hands on you again."

Annie B., bent forward suddenly, cracking up. After seeing my raised eyebrows, she wiped the tears from the corners of her eyes that her humor had formed before explaining, "When your grandmother called me to tell me about that madness, I laughed myself silly. Two days later I caught sight of that same boy giving you a popsicle he'd bought from the bomb-pop man. And you stood there graciously smiling as you accepted his peace offering; right before laying a huge smackaroo square on his lips then skipping away. You all hadn't exchanged one word that whole time. I knew it then and I told your grandmother, you and that boy were MADE for each other."

At that, my grin disappeared. Because, while in some absent-minded way I'd always appreciated Vic and thought he was a cute guy, I never considered him to be anything more than a friend. Something I mentioned as the two women nodded sagely at me.

"I know," Big Mama answered, "though it was something I never really understood. I remember the two times he took some other girl out on a date how unraveled you became. The same thing happened when he left for Purdue your junior year. I mean you were fit to be tied baby girl. There wasn't nothing any of us could say to make you feel better or calm you down. And when I asked you why you were so upset when he was just your friend, you would go on and on about the girl he took out and how she wasn't good enough for him. Or how you'd be losing your Boy-stie since he was going so far away."

My elbows hit my knees and I rested my cheeks in my hands, thinking back. Boy-stie was what I called my "male" best friends, of which there had only been two: Vic and a dude named Maurice. I tried to remember those long-ago high school years, but everything was a blur. The truth is, I don't even remember Vic dating. In fact, I didn't really date either, the more I thought about it. And for the first time in ever, I asked myself why that was? And I really didn't like the answer that I was coming up with as I searched my thoughts.

Whenever Charmaine and I hung out, we did it with a group of friends. We didn't really go out on dates because we didn't have to. I always had Vic there with me, well in my mind, he was with us. And when he'd gone off to Purdue, Maurice. I never needed a guy really since I wasn't interested in getting all serious and mushy with anyone anytime soon.

It's not that I was a late bloomer or that I was saving myself or anything. I was just serious about being successful at whatever it was I found myself ensconced in. I devoted my whole self to a project, whether it was basketball, my courses or an internship, practicum, etc. Whatever I was into, I was about that thing nearly twenty-four hours a day, seven days a week. The last thing I'd needed was some boy in my life thinking he had proprietary rights over my time or activities. So, when boys asked me out, the answer was always no.

I had crushes though. I permitted myself lots of those. But that was it. A crush didn't hijack my time or my commitments. A crush didn't ask me for more than what I was willing to give or to sacrifice my own endeavors for its sake. It just remained there, in the background, waiting for me to indulge in it as I wished. And when I was done with it, I'd pack it back up in its little box until I wanted to play with it again. Something that you could not do with an individual expecting give and take.

I found all these new revelations disturbing. Because, what if I finally found myself ready to embark on a relationship, to devote myself to that as well as my future career, and just happened upon the first available male that caught my eye? What if Rodney wasn't really the person I would have chosen as a mate had Vic been around? What if my whole life, the conception of my children, and the pain I was experiencing today had happened all because Rodney merely came along at the opportune time?

I groaned as my hands went from my cheeks to cover my face.

"There it is," Annie B. grunted.

Keeping my face covered, I shook my head no. I wasn't ready for anymore revelations. I was still mentally masticating the thought that Rodney had just been a warm body that came along when I decided that I wanted a boyfriend.

Ignoring my head shake, Big Mama also grunted before saying all the things I did not want to hear.

"You were always that way baby. You decided that you wanted something, and you wanted it right then. So, you'd go after it, full of determination and focus. You were just like your mama that way. You still are. I remember asking you if you felt like you and Rodney were rushing things a little. You stood your little grown self right there in my kitchen looking me dead in the eye before saying with finality – He's my choice Big Mama, I know what I want, and I want Rodney."

I groaned louder and my face went from my hands to my thighs. I remembered that. I remembered that entire conversation. I suddenly felt sick.

Because, while these revelations were good to finally realize, they didn't help me where Vic was concerned now.

I wasn't in a place in my life where I felt like I could handle another relationship. I could barely handle my day to day life with raising my three kids, working at a job that made me want to commit hari-kari half the time and running a podcast with my crazy friend, all while going through a divorce. I couldn't even keep the frikken white board on the refrigerator up to date. I'd bought that thing 3 years ago with the intent to write cute encouraging phrases, messages or scriptures on it every morning for the kids. I also planned to list the date, the chore for that day and notable events coming up to keep us organized and informed. Yeah. I did all of that for two weeks.

If I couldn't manage a simple goal of updating a stupid whiteboard every morning, how the heck could I handle a budding relationship with all that was going on.

My heart rate increased as I smashed my face further into my legs. A panicky, overwhelming feeling started to rise in my chest and clog my throat. I felt my face and arms get hot and all of a sudden, I felt like I couldn't breathe.

"You stop that right now Naomi Maureen Brooks! I see you. I see you over there making yourself sick with worry. What have I always told you? Answer me girl," Big Mama snapped.

I swallowed hard and took a shaky breath before speaking into my thighs.

"Worry is time wasted fearing something that might never happen."

"That's right. Whatever mess you've got swimming around in that brain of yours, you need to give that to God and get your mind right."

"That's right. Get yourself together, girl! The last thing you need is for your babies to come back in here seeing you pale as a ghost about to pass out," Annie B. added.

I swallowed a mouth full of air that I nearly choked on. They were right of course. I had to get myself together before my babies got back. In all this time, from the moment I'd told Rodney to leave, I never allowed my kids to see me break down once. Their world needed security and stability. And the reality stood that providing that was all on me. So, I did exactly what I needed to do for my babies.

I sat up, wiped my face of the cold sweat that had congealed there and prayed my prayer. While I was no longer a "hater" per se, I found that the prayer I prayed with confidence internally was more about me trusting God to take care of me instead of worrying about others. Or worrying about anything, as it was in this case.

As if on cue, my kiddos came trotting through the door, bursting with information about their afternoon's adventures. And my smile was genuine as I listened in, grabbing my boy onto my lap to give them my full attention. I did this while ignoring the gnawing fear growing in my belly.

Chapter 10

I watched my best friend launch into the next Q and A question with gusto, almost feeling sorry for the caller on the other end (but not really). I mean, we were all about educating the common hater by helping them realize their own purpose and blessing, but this one here? She was on the wrong side of ridiculous.

"… And if you can't accept that what God has for you is for you, you're going to find yourself caught up in the loop of hater-repeat and hater-replay. That's you, mentally rehearsing your current state – what you see, dooming yourself to repeat it verbally."

"That's right, " I interjected, "faith comes by hearing and hearing by the word of God. If faith comes by hearing, how do you think fear comes? Fear is negative faith. That means that it also comes by hearing. Only it's not God's word that you're leaning on."

"We're saying all of that to say, if you don't want to find yourself in the vicious cycle of repeating your haterisms and replaying your defeats and failures, you're going to have to change what you say and why you say it." Maine added.

"Yes, ma'am. But what can't happen," I had to mention, "is you following your past around like it still owns you. Your ex-dude is your EX for a reason. Stop worrying about his new family and new life without you. God gave you the key to the shackles and pointed the way to peace. It's up to you to unlock the chains, step out of them and let them fall. Or you'll find that, even if the chains aren't holding you, you might be holding on to them."

"Because quiet as kept, we all tend to look for the excuse of why we can't move forward," Charmaine said somberly, "when the sad truth is, we really don't want to. Whether it's out of fear or because we are lazy. It's much easier to remain where we are in life and blame somebody or something else for it."

I paused as I heard the caller break down. I wanted to let it go at that. I wanted to encourage her now and let her know that we've all been there, but there was one more thing I had to make sure she understood.

"You are required to do better. Because you know better. God has so much for you in this life, right now; and you're too busy holding onto the crap He told you to let go of a long time ago. It's time to make a choice, girlfriend. Either you're going to spend the rest of your life talking about it..."

"Or just BE about it and get the dang thing done," Charmaine finished.

We held on then, fully understanding what our sister on the line was going through. The main pitfall of transitioning from a hater to a reformed hater was arriving at "the choice". If you didn't take your life by the reigns and step up into your God-given talents and strengths, you would invariably end up being stepped on by raw and lacerated emotions, constantly bombarding you about other people and other things that you cannot change.

Charmaine started the prayer and I joined in.

"Father, God, In the name of Christ Jesus, we know that you see us. You hear us and you love us. You knew and approved us in our mother's wombs. You know the count of every hair on our head and know the content of every thought in our heart. You are ours and we are yours. Help us see what you see, say what you say, and be everything you need us to be. Your ways are higher than our ways and your thoughts are higher than our thoughts. We trust you with the pain of our past and rely on your direction for our future. Order our steps and direct our paths straight. How can we hate our brother or sister, a creation in your image? How can we not love them and say we love you, whom we can't see? Thank you for the forgiveness of our sins, we confess love and not hate; forgiving, we let go of the pain. You are Alpha and Omega. We trust you fully and completely to provide. Because what's for us is for US. In the name of Jesus our Lord we pray, Amen."

The caller thanked us profusely, but I barely heard her words. Instead, I heard echoing in my own heart that I needed to start "practicing what I preached".

That was the thing about God's word. It was a double-edged sword that cuts both coming and going. So, while we were giving our sister God's take on worry and fear, it was delivering the same blows or truth to my own little self. And I'd learned long ago not to ignore God's messages, whether they were for someone else or for me.

Mentally promising to take all of that into account, I focused on using the remainder of the broadcast to let our listeners know about our new swag, Hater-cation line of t-shirts and the possibility of a new show on Pure-flix.

Finished with the wrap up I noticed that Maine had grown unusually quiet.

"You okay over there?"

Her sad grin was telling. The fear that I had just promised God I'd let go gripped me.

"Is Big Mama okay?"

Maine's eyebrows went up as her mouth formed a perfect "O" of surprise.

"Uh... yeah, she's good."

I sighed in relief and suddenly felt so weak I wanted to fall to the floor. For the first time in I can't remember when, I saw my best friend hesitate before asking,

"Is Destiny okay?"

I sighed again. This time in resignation. Because the short answer was no. The long answer? No, my sister was not okay. No, my sister wouldn't be okay for a long time. And no, I had no idea what to do or how to help her.

We'd learned this evening after my visit with Annie B. and before the podcast that Destiny had well and truly been fired. There was some gibberish about some moral turpitude clause in her contract and how that clause was breached by the video gone viral of what we now called the Ice Club debacle.

Add that to Mike still not taking her calls and the fact that news of the video and ongoing investigations was now being mentioned on a few local news outlet webpages, our outlook on the whole Destiny front was bleak.

Maine being who she was to me, I gave her the long answer. As bad as things were and as horrible as I felt about them, I was still surprised when Maine's gaze turned soft and watery. An observation that only confirmed the truth as I knew it. Maine used her former attraction of Mike and supposed bitterness of his relationship with my sister as a front. What I couldn't figure out though was why?

Whatever the reason, I smiled sadly at my bestie before reminding her of what we'd just said in ministry to our sister and how it applied to us as well.

Maine nodded her agreement, hugged me with the promise of chatting tomorrow, and headed out without me.

Usually we walked out together when a podcast was done. But Vic's presence beside the radio room door sent an unspoken message to the both of us that he and I needed to have words.

I frowned, watching him close the door behind my best friend before heading to where I remained, seated at the table.

I swallowed hard because I could read Vic like a book. And since our past couple encounters featured his flirty fun side along with his being about business visage – the way he moved and the frown on his face currently sent a whole other message. Vic was frustrated. Vic was beyond frustrated. And apparently, I wasn't going to be able to leave until I found out why.

***

Vic...

He'd been watching Naomi all night, doing what God created her to do, despite the hell that was breaking lose in her life. Vic had always been impressed at her resilience and determination. But he had to admit, with everything that had gone down, he'd been surprised to see her and Maine tonight, there on time to go live as usual.

And since he'd tried to give them space after what Destiny had gone through, he hadn't been by the house or called. But that didn't mean that he wasn't worried about them. And he had been. Extremely worried.

As far as he was concerned, this had all gone down on his watch. A woman, a FRIEND had been assaulted in his club. More than that, these were people that were close to him, people that he'd made a vow at one time or another to protect and keep safe.

Guilt gnawed at him as he again saw a replay of that video in his mind. He could feel his forehead crease as he ground his teeth. The video had been burned into his brain and he couldn't help his visceral reaction to it, despite how he could see Naomi perceiving his demeanor as something other than it was by her own panicked facial expression.

Attempting to calm his mind and redirect his thoughts, Vic took a calming breath before pulling a chair around to sit face to face with his girl. The news that he had to deliver to her now, on top of all that she was going through, was far from pleasant. That being the case, he decided that the quicker he got around to delivering it, the better.

"Rodney came by the station today."

Naomi blinked rapidly. And though Vic knew he managed to throw her with that revelation, he thought it best to continue quickly so that she could digest the information all at once.

"He asked a lot of questions, including "in my opinion," what was an estimate on the donations and clothing sales for *Hater-cation*. He also had questions about how much you were charged for room use during the podcast and what type of cut was Maine's takeaway."

Watching her pupils dilate as her gaze narrowed and the sides of her mouth tightened, Vic hated that he had to be the one to deliver that little bit of trash.

Because his visit with Rodney hadn't been at all pleasant. First, it had been completely unexpected. Second, Vic did NOT like that guy. So, when he'd heard his name yelled from behind him in the voice that he near despised, he'd tensed before turning to face Rodney head on.

"Hey man, what's up. How're you doing?" Rodney faked, reaching out to take Vic's hand before giving him the quick "hug in, back pound, release" greeting.

"Hey," Vic answered, stepping back two quick paces before leaning on his trucks grill, arms folded.

Rodney glanced behind him like he was making sure he wasn't seen. Vic tensed at that.

"Um, so hey..." Rodney began.

"Yeah man, you said that. You mind getting to the point? I've got stuff to do."

"Right, riiigghhht."

Vic heard Naomi go "ugh" in his head. It was an "ugh" he firmly agreed with as he forced himself to patiently wait for Rodney to make his play, whatever that play might be.

"So yeah," Rodney continued, "I just had a few questions about Naomi's podcast that I was hoping you had a minute to answer. I would ask her you know, but this divorce thang got her all bitter and silly acting. You know how women can be right?" Rodney chuckled.

"No." Vic answered shortly. Was this guy serious?

"Right, right. I know you all grew up together so you're friends. Friends don't see that side of one another you know what I'm saying?"

"No." Vic answered again, this time with exasperation mixed in. His patience was waning fast.

Rodney, obviously having picked up on Vic's less than receptive attitude, hurried on.

"Okay, okay. Well, me and my wife don't get along right now. So, you know, if I ask her a few questions about the podcast or how well its doing, she won't answer. I only ask because I really care about her and I know how important it is to her you know? I still love her, man. She's still my wife and I want her happy. The only problem I have is the amount of time she spends doing it. Time she should be devoting to raising my kids so..."

Vic grunted, and palmed his key fob to flip the locks on his truck. Turning and walking around to the driver side door, he opened it, tossed in his gym bag and closed it again before turning to face the man he tried hard not to snarl at.

"What did you need to know?"

And that's when Rodney had shown his hand. Thinking back on the whole conversation, Vic shook his head in confusion. He'd had no idea why Rodney, knowing that Vic and Naomi were friends, would think that he'd tell him anything?

Something he revealed to Naomi now.

Naomi blinked at him; her furrowed brow indicating that she was probably just as confused as he was.

"Does he think you're stupid?" She asked, breaking the silence finally.

Vic hunched his shoulders in answer. In his mind, he didn't even want to know what a guy like that would be thinking. To understand him would mean having the capacity to think like him. To Vic, that was not a complimentary line of thought.

"Okay," Naomi sighed.

Vic watched her shoulders haunch in seeming defeat. His girl was tired. And seeing that frustrated him even more. Resigning himself to having another chat with Zee about what his options were on dealing with Rodney, he reached forward and softly grabbed her face in his hands.

Before he realized what he was doing, he landed a soft kiss on her lips, then her eyes and finally her forehead, all before leaning his forehead against hers.

"God got this, Naomi. Don't doubt Him. And don't worry. Rodney's looking for an angle, a way to turn this divorce thing in his favor. He's a con man, baby. Nothing good can come of whatever it is he's planning."

Naomi's hands wrapped around his on each side of her face. She squeezed them, her only answer to his encouragement. With her eyes still closed, Vic wondered where her head was at. Loosening his hold to let go and relax back into his seat, he felt her hands tighten on to hold them to her face as her eyes opened.

Seeing the torment swirling in their depths, Vic oddly wished that she'd kept them closed; allowing him the illusion that she was okay. But she wasn't okay. Not one bit.

He opened his mouth to say something; anything that might help, when her next words interrupted, making it clear that Rodney was not the reason for that look in her eyes.

"Vic... we need to talk. We need to talk about us."

He felt his body jerk with shock, the impact of her words coupled with the sorrow in her gaze making his gut twist. A man that had never really known fear in his life suddenly found himself face to face with it. He'd waited for Naomi... for this... his entire life it seemed. And losing it; losing the potential of what they could

have once she and Rodney were all said and
done was not an option.

C. Marie Evans

Chapter 11

Destiny

She heard the door close behind Nahmi and the kids. And sighed in relief.

Watching them watch her with worry that increased more and more every day, Destiny wanted to get her mind and heart right. She wanted to be okay and for them to know that, no matter what had happened the last week to completely shred her life; she was going to be alright.

But she wasn't alright. And, thanks to her family and all those lovely teachings on integrity, she couldn't even pretend like she was. She didn't know how. What was worse, she didn't have the energy to do it anyway.

Every time she even thought about getting out of bed the events of the past week came flooding back in a storm of visual torture, beginning with her deciding to go to Club Ice after her and Mike's first fight.

Well, it hadn't been a fight exactly, just what she felt was a small disagreement. As in she disagreed with his take on her spending so much time around her family. And, she'd disagreed with his not wanting to drop her at the hospital to check on Annie B. And last, she'd disagreed with his expectation that, "When we get married, you're going to have to narrow your focus. Your career, your family, all of that will be based on whatever firm I decide is best for us. I've got my eye on the east coast. You might as well start preparing now by cutting some of those crazy cousins of yours loose."

And, while Destiny had always been laid back when it came to their relationship. The fact was, most choices made during the relationship didn't matter to her. And those things that didn't matter? She didn't bother to argue or fuss about. So, when Mike wanted Chinese food for the third time in a week instead of what she'd cooked for dinner? She'd pack up the food and use it for lunch the next couple of days.

Or, when Mike decided they needed a night in because he was tired when they'd made plans with friends. She'd call them and make their excuses. It hadn't bothered her that much. In fact, she felt as if she was looking after her future husband and seeing to his needs.

But everyone had a limit. And Destiny's family was hers. Her family was the only time that she and Mike truly disagreed. Even when he had a problem with one of her correspondence trips, she'd work with her editors to make sure that the dates and times were flexible so they wouldn't interfere with whatever events he had scheduled.

It was when his comments started targeting Naomi that Destiny had to admit… she'd grown a bit nasty.

"And that uppity sister of yours. She's just a social worker with a podcast yet she acts like she's Michelle Obama or something. The best thing about leaving this state is getting you away from her and those kids. If you ask me, her opinion means way too much to you."

"But I didn't ask you. And just because you grew up an only child without any cousins or real friends, that doesn't mean that mine are expendable. My sister has always been there for me when I needed her. Always. And if any female on this planet can compare to Michelle Obama, it's her. So, keep your mouth off my family Michael Wallace. When it comes to anything else, you know I have your back. But you try to come between me and my family, you can leave the state by yourself."

She'd felt so good about her little speech that night. And it had seemed like perfect timing when Lindsay had called her to invite her out to Club Ice. Getting away from Michael and his aspersions against her family had seemed like a good idea. Feeling liberated, Destiny had donned her best little black dress and her response when Michael had asked her where she was going?

"Out."

And that had been the end of that. The end of everything.

The tears started again. Grabbing the box of tissue from the nightstand, Destiny found the huge container empty; it was a find that caused a whole other torrent of tears to fall because could absolutely nothing go right in her life?

On cue, her cell phone began to play the soundtrack from I-Carly, her and Lindsay's favorite Nickelodeon show when they were kids, now Lindsay's ring tone.

A ringtone Destiny ignored again. Because she was beyond pissed at her best friend. And yes, she was probably being a tad unfair. But whatever. If Lindsay hadn't suggested they go out to the club that night, her life wouldn't be in shambles right now.

About to roll over and do what helped her best forget the mess her life had become, another ringtone sounded. One that had her bolting upright and grabbing desperately for the phone.

Interrupting the song, *A Whole New World*, she fumbled the phone before finally getting a grip to slam it against her ear.

"Mike?" Her voice was hesitant as was the response she received.

Finally, "We need to talk," sounded from the other end of the connection.

True to his style of communication. Mike cut right to the point in his "bull in a china shop" fashion, not one to complain however, especially within the current circumstances, Destiny found herself responding in kind.

"When? And where do you want to meet."

***

Vic

He threw the pillow right off the couch and watched it hit the wall with a puff before falling to the floor.

Not satisfied, he threw the other one, feeling a little better as it followed the path of the first.

"Feel better?" Zee snorted, glancing up briefly from some nonsense he was working on at his desktop before refocusing on his monitor.

"No." Vic grunted.

Zee deep sighed. It was the elderly sibling kind of sigh, almost similar to the sigh of a put-upon parent though not quite the same.

"Are we going to talk about this or are you just going to keep throwing pillows at the wall like the juvenile you used to be not too long ago."

And Vic didn't know what irritated him more. That his brother basically just insulted him by calling him immature, or that he hadn't glanced at him once the whole time he did it.

If he wanted juvenile, Vic would give him just that.

The smaller toss pillow glanced off the side of the monitor, gaining Vic his brother's exasperated gaze.

"Really?"

Vic snickered by way of response. Leaning back, he rested both arms along the back of the sofa in his brother's office. The now "pillow free" sofa.

Zee shook his head, punched some keys and after a few clicks of his mouse, he got up, walked around his desk so that he could half sit, half lean on the front of it directly in front of Vic, just 8 feet from where he was sitting.

He crossed his arms and one leg over the other, almost like he was settling in for the long haul.

"What happened?"

Vic grunted again before glancing to his right to concentrate on absolutely nothing just outside the window.

"Okay, I'll be more specific. What happened between you and Naomi?"

Vic felt his gaze snap to his brother's very observant one and suddenly, felt like he'd been thrown back in time to when they were teenagers, him sitting on his brother's bed tossing a ball in the air while Zee had leaned on his desk almost in the exact same stance. Asking him the exact same question.

"It's that obvious?" Vic had to ask.

Zee laughed, shaking his head in what Vic assumed was disbelief. He couldn't blame his brother as; it really was a stupid question. Of course, it was "that obvious."

"Do I need to ask it again or are you going to spit it out? Because I don't have all day..."

Vic snorted again. Because, despite how busy Zee was, his brother had always and will always, move heaven and earth to be there for him or AJ if they ever needed him. Ergo, Vic knew that he could sit there all day and not say a thing, Zee would still be there ready and waiting when he was willing to talk.

Out of respect for the fact that his brother really was just as busy (if not busier) than he was, Vic aired his frustration.

"Naomi wants to stay friends."

He watched Zee's back go stiff, the only indication that his brother had a reaction to what he'd just said.

"She said that?"

"Yeah man, she said that." Vic glanced back out the window, suddenly wanting to be anywhere but in that room.

"I mean, she said that to you, directly? Those were her exact words?"

Vic's gaze flashed in Zee's direction before bouncing back toward the window where it stayed. He sighed and responded in a "don't make me lose my patience" tone, "I paraphrased."

Zee nodded, at least Vic assumed that's the movement he saw him make out of the corner of his eye. He didn't say anything for a minute. Vic waited. He knew from experience that he wasn't done.

"Okay then. Do you remember her exact words? Try not to paraphrase or give me what you think she meant by what she said, I'd like to know what she actually said."

"She said she just wasn't ready for things to grow more serious between us. She added some nonsense about a white board in her house and how her kids have been in a constant state of confusion. She's comfortable with us the way we are. Oh, and she said she won't lie, that she'd always thought I was an attractive guy, but she didn't expect anything more from me besides friendship."

Vic knew he was rambling, shooting those words out staccato style, but he just wanted them gone; out of his memory, out of his life. He just wanted to forget the last month ever happened to tell the truth. He'd rather it never happened then to sit there constantly feeling like someone had sucker punched him in the stomach.

"Got it. And just to be clear, when she stated that she didn't expect anything more from you besides friendship, do you know if she meant in the past or at this present time in her life?'

Vic opened his mouth to give the answer on the top of his head, "Now, stupid," but as his mouth opened, no words came out. Not realizing that his mouth was sitting there hanging open, Vic pondered how, he'd been so wrapped up in Naomi's rejecting where they both obviously wanted to go, that he'd assumed it was how she felt about them now; not just in the past.

"Exactly what I thought. Man, you always do that. You assume you know where the conversation is going, think that you heard what you expected to hear and then make your decisions from there. You need to have another talk with her."

Vic was shaking his head "no" before Zee had ended his sentence. It wasn't that he was giving up or anything. Naomi was going through. She was tired and she was confused. He was more upset about her pulling back because he couldn't help her as much if she remained distant than he was about her thinking that they should just be friends.

"Why no?" Zee asked, looking as if he were trying hard not to roll his eyes like mom used to do.

"Because Naomi's just trying to deal right now, the best way she can. Her head is all jacked up. I'm good. I just have to figure out how to help her, whether she wants me to or not."

"Are you listening to yourself" Zee asked. It was his turn to shake his head, but more along the lines of the same disbelief category as before.

Vic redirected his attention back to the window. It was time to change the subject.

"Heard from AJ?"

Vic could see out of the corner of his eye that Zee's attention had turned to the same window his was directed out of. His brother's chest moved in and then out before he responded.

"Yeah. He came by with the specs and plans for the new buildings in North Carolina and Florida. He's still pissed at you, by the way."

Vic grunted. "I kinda got that when he didn't show up to raid my fridge all week. Where's he eating anyway?"

"Are you kidding?" Zee laughed. "You owe me two weeks' worth of groceries, man."

Vic laughed, rose out of his seat, then headed toward the far wall to retrieve the tossed pillows.

"Aye man, I'm serious. That boy eats like two football teams. When I asked him where all my food had gone in the last week, you know what he told me? That it wasn't his fault he was once a preemie and had to make up for lost time."

Vic's guffaw paused him in his tracks. Holding the three pillows to himself, he was helpless to do anything but bend over and hold tight to them until the laughter passed. His younger brother needed some serious help. But the boy was funny. He had to give him that.

Getting ahold of himself, Vic tossed the three pillows back on the couch before turning toward his disgruntled elder sibling and responding.

"This is your fault. You shouldn't have played all those practical jokes on us when we were kids. You had that boy drinking out of the toilet talking about, 'Toilet water...it's so refreshing.' It's your turn now bruh. You reap what you sow."

Saying that while he was still laughing, Vic headed toward the door. He wasn't surprised, even a little, when he felt all three pillows hit him in the back. All of which just made him laugh even harder.

Chapter 12

Naomi
St.   Louis   County   Court   House
Division 21

Glancing nervously toward the door, I checked my watch again. Freda was late. And that was unusual. So unusual, that I don't remember the last time that she was late for anything. With my mind blowing her tardiness out of proportion, by the time my imagination was done, she'd been kidnapped by pirates, taken by human traffickers and had been given a pair of concrete boots by the same mob that ghosted Jimmy Hoffa.

Reluctantly, I turned to face the front of the room again. I say reluctant because I hated this room. Hate as in knock down, dragged out, spit in your face kinda hate. I guess I expected the court room to look like it did on television. I distinctly remember the court room in the movie "Liar Liar" with Jim Carry looking way nicer than this one.

This was the type of room that ugly tapestry and quilts would go to die in. It was reasonably clean; I would give them that... but that was about all it had going for it. Despite its utter ugliness, the room was rich with a mixture of new and old-style design, though a renovation had happened of the entire complex recently.

Or maybe I was just uncomfortable, thus projecting how I felt every time that I was in the room upon the room itself. And I was always uncomfortable in here, for so many reasons. Reason number one: I hated sitting in audience seats like a spectator to people that were NOT ME, debating on how my life and my kids' lives would function from here on out. Reason number two? Every court date, like clockwork, Rodney brought *her*. Personally, I didn't dislike or like the woman. I felt absolutely nothing about her. My problem was her modeling short shorts in front of my kids (and even shorter skirts in front of me on court days). And, to be truthful, my true problem was her being there somehow always making me feel like I was in this alone.

I knew that God was in that room with me and that if God was with me, he was more than the world against me. But that didn't change the way I feel when I glanced over to their side of the room, watching them take their stand as a united front against the world (and me). For some reason, the whole scenario reminded me of David and Goliath. I hadn't realized that until Charmaine had regurgitated one of Annie B.'s old teachings from when we were kids, "Chile, people work harder to live their lives looking like life is perfect. They put more work into looking like they've got it all instead of putting in the work to just BE and have it all. So, believe half of what you see and none of what you hear babies, because people lie with their very lives all day long."

Before remembering that lesson, they seemed so much bigger than me; a united front, like the great wall of Rodney.

And now? Only slightly so. Learning to check my emotions at the door had been the hardest lesson of this whole stupid love gone wrong experiment. But maybe that's what God wanted me to learn from all of this. Or maybe I just needed to accept that, should I spend the rest of my life alone (well not alone, I would always have my kids and my family) or without a mate, maybe this was part of that process. A process where I learned that I didn't need a mate to complete me. I'm not saying that it wouldn't be nice to have a guy around to do the things I don't like such as taking out the trash, mowing the lawn and the like. But I was my mother's daughter. Meaning, I wasn't waiting around for some Prince Charming to ride up on his prized steed to rescue me. I'd be saving myself, thank you very much. And if that meant cutting the grass during allergy season while my skin turned purple with rashes in response, I'd just pick up some calamine lotion and keep it pushing.

That was the last thought in my head before all coherent thought vaporized. One of Freda's associates from her law office was approaching me. I don't remember the lady's name, but I did recall that she was a nice lady... with man hands. Not that having man hands was bad... it just creeped me out a little since the woman in question was a tiny redhead with a perky personality and sing song voice.

"Good Morning Naomi. Freda just called. There was a slight mishap with her car, but she's got it handled and is on her way so just sit tight okay?"

I nodded my okay while mentally pushing down the frustration building inside of me. At least she wasn't kidnapped by pirates. I mentally chuckled at my own foolishness before I felt the hair on the back of my neck stand on end.

Trying to appear casual and bored, I allowed my gaze to complete a circuit around the courtroom, starting with the judge. I took in the left side of the room, noting two other people that were sitting far removed from each other while staring daggers from their end of the benches. Obviously, a divorcing pair, I briefly wondered why they would sit on the same side, the same bench even, while giving each other the stink eye. They had to have been the cutest couple. The guy was Asian, and the lady was black. If they sued for divorce on Divorce Court the television show, that judge would send them home on a 6-month trial reconciliation. They didn't want to be divorced. The love between them was still very powerful and practically assaulted me across the aisle. Praying silently for them that they figure it out

151

before it was too late, I allowed my gaze to wander further to the back.

Where it collided with a dark, intense gaze; so familiar to me that I should have known that he was the cause.

Vic's little side grin appeared as he chin-upped his acknowledgment of my surprise. Without thinking, I mouthed, "Come here," with squinted eyes, after which I felt my mouth go from its wide-open gape to a tight, pursed expression that spoke volumes.

The half grin became a full one as his long legs propelled his body upward and out of the bench.

I gulped. And again, lost track of all coherent thought. Making all black look like the style was created just for him, Vic prowled – yes, he did... *prowled* to my bench where, for some reason, I felt myself sitting up just a little taller; my back was just a little bit straighter while my heart nearly beat itself out of my chest.

And did he sit down like every other person in the room with common sense? No. He did not. Instead, he leans over from the end of the bench while placing one hand on the back of it and the other across me to rest on the seat just beside my right hip. His face was so close that I could feel his breath on my lips. Which meant I forgot how to breathe or even form a thought. Licking my bottom lip nervously I suddenly forgot how inappropriate it would be if Vic were to kiss me right there in front of the judge and everybody. And as his dark gaze captured mine once again, I fell right into its cavernous depths. I didn't care about Rodney, about the judge and didn't even remember my cousin err attorney's name. I was completely enraptured by all that was Victavious.

I was so caught up in his haze of male goodness that I almost missed his grin before I watched his mouth form words; that, in this moment had to be the most important thing in my world besides my God and my kids.

"What?" I breathed, having missed whatever he'd said, anticipating it with such longing that my entire body was strung tight in expectancy.

"I said, scootch over."

***

Vic

It took every ounce of control that he had not to laugh at Naomi's peeved expression. No, wait... it had taken every ounce of control to keep from gloating at her surprised, open-mouthed gape when she caught sight of him sitting in the back of the room. Now, he was way past self-control, depending solely on the strength of the Almighty to keep from laughing in the face of her irritation.

Why it felt like it had been forever since he'd last seen her, he had no idea. But he knew a couple of things.

First, while he hadn't been through a divorce, his older brother had. Watching a man that, even as a teenager practically personified the words strength and control, break down over the entire ordeal had nearly been his family's undoing. And through that entire torturous process one thing his brother told him stood out in his memory: "I've never felt so alone than when I stood up in that courtroom. Despite my attorney, despite the judge, despite everyone else that sent messages of love and encouragement, it was one of the most intimidating moments in my entire life. I have never felt like God deserted me. Until that moment."

The thought of Naomi feeling like that made Vic sick to his stomach. A sick feeling that drove him to finding out her next court date and making it a point to be there. His psyche had argued that Freda would be there, and that Naomi didn't need him. And he didn't care. At all. He'd be there, just in case.

He'd gotten there late, but that didn't matter since there seemed to be a delay, some other mishap no doubt that worked in his favor. Glancing toward the ceiling to acknowledge the One that always worked things together for his good, he finally took his seat next to Naomi after she huffed and puffed for a good fifteen seconds (and yeah, he counted) before scooting over.

He ignored his body's physical reaction to her eyes going all dreamy. He'd been so close to forgetting about them being in a public court room. So close to showing her how her nonsensical argument used to keep him at bay couldn't possibly hold up. This thing that had been present within him since they were kids had ensnared them both. He'd already lost his battle with it a long time ago. He'd come to accept that Naomi was that one; not perfect by any means, but perfect for him. And sooner or later, she'd come to that same conclusion.

"What are you doing here?"

Giving her a side glance with a hint of a grin that he couldn't hold back, Vic refocused on what had captured his attention the moment he'd planted his behind in the seat.

Rodney. For a man that seemed so happy to be divorcing and moving on, he definitely didn't look pleased at the aspect that Naomi would eventually do the same. Sinister, malevolent and violent energy emanated from him in waves that Vic couldn't see. But he could feel them. Rodney's dark gaze held his for a few more seconds before the woman to his left turned his face toward her as she spoke.

If Vic had hackles, they'd all be standing on edge. Every male instinct in him made him aware that he'd just been threatened. And every male instinct in him hungered to answer that challenge.

"Victavious!"

Determined to answer the call of that nonsense later, Vic turned sideways to give Naomi his full attention.

"Why is it that every woman alive has this raw talent. You all have a way of saying a man's name that changes the meaning of it like a chameleon. Say my name in bed, and it becomes an aphrodisiac. Say it with a smile, it becomes flirtatious. Say it with a frown, like you're doing now, and it becomes a chastisement."

Vic derived pure satisfaction from watching her blink as he was sure she had no answer to that before adding, "Let's test that theory, shall we? How about when we get out of here, we go back to my place and test them in that order – bed, smile and back to frown again?"

Trying not to laugh, he watched her frown fade only to be followed by that dreamy look he liked so much. A look that influenced him in a way that he couldn't explore publicly. His body was already preparing to run this one in for a touch-down. Vic's mind, however, was throwing several flags on that play, one of which was attached to a "You're in a courtroom, moron," sign.

Grace had to be his friend today. Vic thought and accepted this as truth since he was about to get himself a taste of that mouth again, public or no, before he felt his body being jolted back.

A very feminine yet muscular arm (one that he remembered well from a few beat downs as a kid) reached across him to flatten him against the back of the bench.

"Hey girl," Freda was saying in her rushed, sing-song voice. A voice that oddly suited her.

"I am so sorry, had to clean up after changing my flat tire and yes, of course I would pop a flat tire on my way to court because, my life what? Sucks, that's what. How you doing? You okay? He didn't say anything to you, did he? Because if he did..."

Vic closed his eyes briefly on his deep sigh, shaking his head at the way Naomi's cousins treated her and Destiny. From the moment the girls' father had passed away, the rest of the family had taken it upon themselves to protect the girls (then, now women). And they took that role seriously. So seriously in fact, Vic knew people personally that had been hospitalized for even mentioning Naomi or Destiny in an unkind fashion. Not to mention his own run-ins with "the cousins".

And while Freda's protection was overbearing as in still overbearing even though Naomi was over thirty years old; her mode of protectiveness was sweet. Now Elaine, she was straight up frightening. He couldn't believe that the woman still carried a knife on her! There was always that one crazy cousin. Vic figured that Elaine fit that label to a tee.

Naomi rushed to assure Freda that all was well. Freda finished up her briefing quickly, flashed a warning look his way, then headed toward the front of the court room where she was met halfway by the tiny red head he'd seen talking to Naomi earlier.

"Are you going to answer me sometime today?"

Back to this. Vic sighed and crossed his arms over his chest. He watched with interest as Freda's back straightened when the lady pulled out a file and flipped through some papers to bring out a sheet that Freda all but snatched out of her hand.

"Dude, are you just going to ignore me."

Vic leaned forward, his focus sharpening as Freda angrily marched back toward them.

"Outside." She shot out as she moved past their bench and headed toward the back of the court room and out the door.

Vic turned to Naomi and watched her mimic his own "blinking-in-confusion stare" before he hopped up and pulled her by the hand toward the exit. Freda was mad. Beyond mad, actually. As in, he hadn't seen her this mad since the time she'd socked him in the nose for trying to kiss Naomi on the cheek when he was twelve.

He and Naomi hit the door at a near run. Scanning the hallway briefly, he caught sight of

Freda pacing at the other end. Allowing Naomi to go before him, he held tightly to her hand.

"What..." Naomi couldn't even get her question out before Freda blew.

"I do not BELIEVE this shiftless negro! The nerve. The freaking audacity! I should call Elaine. I should let her have her way with him and do my best to keep her out of prison!"

Okay. If Vic hadn't been worried before, he was really worried now.

Naomi must have shared his sentiment as she did something they all had learned never to do; interrupt one of Freda's rants.

"Tell me Free! What's happening?"

Freda's back was to them now as she'd been in the "retreat" part of her pacing. Shaking her head as if she were disagreeing with herself, she executed a perfect military turn and handed me the paper.

As I read it, she explained.

"That is a document that idiot wants to file with the court today. He's asking that a Quadro be executed for all funds that you have in investments, 401-K and savings. He's looking for evidence to support his request to the court that your earnings are supplemented with donations, gifts and profits that you receive from the podcast and Hater's prayer merchandise."

"Okay," Naomi nodded, her shoulders dropping as she sighed in what he guessed was relief. Vic's hand clenched hers tightly, letting her know the best way he could that Freda wasn't done.

"We expected that right? That's not going to be a problem once I show them where my share of that money goes right? We talked about this..."

"That's not all, Nahmi." Freda's teeth were gritted as she said that last part.

And so were Vic's. In fact, if it wouldn't kill Naomi's case against the punk, he'd already be in that court room punching the idiot repeatedly.

"Okay, so what? What is it?"

Naomi glanced at Vic. Vic knew she guessed from his expression that it was all bad as he felt her hand clutch his in a death grip.

"He's requested a guardian ad-litem for the kids. He's seeking full custody. Apparently, he reached out to a school counselor last week...?"

"Beth Riverside, right?"

Freda paused. Her eyes narrowed and her nose flared before she exhaled and asked, "Why do you know her name as if something happened between you?"

"Beth made it a habit of flirting openly with Rodney throughout our marriage. It got to the point where she did this right in front of my face as if I didn't exist or didn't matter. She would never address me during meetings and was downright rude whenever I called with questions about the kids. Finally, I'd had enough of that madness. Two of the teachers had witnessed her treatment of me and supported my complaint to the principal. I was assured that she was reprimanded appropriately, and should I ever have that experience with her in any way to let the school know. I haven't had any, but there has really been no need to talk with her directly lately."

"There's been a need Naomi. She just hasn't told you..."

Vic felt Naomi stiffen. He knew the signs to watch for and steeled himself to catch hold of her if he had to. Sure enough, the tips of her ears turned red. That always happened first. Followed by her face and neck growing flushed. He could feel her pulse through her hand as her hold tightened, gripping him so hard he had to clench his teeth to hold back a grunt. But he didn't ask her to let go. This was about her kids. Everyone that was anyone knew that one thing that could not ever happen was to withhold information from Naomi about her kids.

"Finish." Naomi growled. Freda knew the signs too. She'd already walked around to the other side of us, blocking the way that led back to the courtroom.

"Nahmi."

"Fi-nish!" She almost shouted it. Freda's mouth worked as she tried to find the words. And because it was taking her too long to get it out, Vic did so to put both out of their misery.

"Attached is a report from the counselor. Madison has been called in to the office and sent to the nurse three times in the last two weeks. The counselor has stated that she conferenced with the parents, you in particular, about her concern regarding Madison's mental health. She's written here that, because you've taken no action to assist your child, a protective services call has been placed to child services on Madison's behalf."

Naomi blinked at the obvious lie before she jerked her hand from mine. Moving past the lie part that probably mattered but not nearly as much as Madison, she zoomed in on that issue.

"What is it? What's wrong with my baby? What hasn't she told me?"

Vic answered with no hesitation.

"It's suspected that she's cutting, baby. There are scars on her arms and legs that she's inked over or covered with designs, according to the report. She's told the counselor that she's not doing it. But her friends have told a few teachers otherwise. There is also a concern here… Baby…"

"Tell me." Naomi cried.

Hating the pain that he was causing her but wanting to get her what she needed as quickly as he could, Vic finished in a rush.

"There are signs that she is severely depressed, Baby. Possibly even suicidal."

Vic dropped the sheet and grabbed hold just in time to take Naomi's agonizing scream into his chest. Her jerking sobs were so powerful he had to brace to keep them standing.

Rage burned within him so strongly, Vic held tight to Naomi while clenching his fists at her back. Over her head, his gaze burned into Freda's. His spoke volumes beginning and ending with the message that she'd better fix this or that he damn sure would. And Freda's gaze burned right back into his, assuring him with a protectiveness he knew would take care of his woman. She was going to make Rodney pay for that. And Vic was going to let her. Because he had some unfinished business with an elementary school counselor.

Chapter 13

Annie B.
St. Luke's Hospital
2 days after surgery

Annie B. blinked away the fog from the pain meds and focused. She knew she'd see her there. Her best friend for life. It was fitting that she'd be there with her in the end.

And Annie knew it was coming soon, knew it was the end. Oh, she'd fought it. She was a soldier. A survivor. It was just unnatural for her to lay down and say Boo, even to death when it came knocking. But it would have her in the end. Of that she had no doubt.

Cora sat there, falling asleep in her chair, her sudoku puzzle near sliding off her lap. Annie shook her head groggily. She remembered asking Cora why she wasted her time on that mess.

"Keeps my mind active so I remember your name. You should be grateful. Without this here book, I'd be walking around calling you 'friend' cause I can't remember much else."

Annie had laughed then and chuckled now. They had a lot of laughs in their day. And a lot of tears. But through the loss, the pain, the fun times and the hard ones, since they'd met that day over forty-eight years ago, they'd never been farther from each other than around the corner.

It was a state of being they'd passed on to their grandchildren, this friendship that was the same as kinship. And Annie was so grateful to God almighty for giving her that gift.

So how was she supposed to tell Cora goodbye? And worse, how was she to tell Charmaine? Her grandbaby wouldn't understand. Annie could feel the life being pulled from her daily with each breath she took. And she knew without a doubt, that were she to let these two know, they'd tell her to shut that madness up and have faith.

They wouldn't understand. Understand what she knew deep in her bones. And, despite knowing, she fought every day to remain. Because Charmaine just wasn't ready.

Her girl was grown, no doubt. And her smile often shown like the sun, a very real source of joy for Annie. But her baby was broken too. Not irretrievably so, but still. Charmaine lived her life on a precipice of pretense. To say she'd had a hard life would be putting it mildly. And if Annie hadn't stepped in to take her grandbaby into her own home to raise her after that fateful night, she knew her granddaughter wouldn't be here today.

While Charmaine had learned that she was safe once again with Annie, the pain never left her and it never healed. She just became a professional at hiding it. She wasn't ready for this kind of loss. So, Annie argued with God. She fought the pull of the inevitable. She woke every day in deep pain, her strength draining just from her struggle to remain.

It hadn't been a surprise to her, when Dr. Maxwell had come in that morning to explain that there were complications. It hadn't frightened her either. His demeanor had gone from hesitant to baffled at her nodding acceptance. Because he hadn't told her anything she didn't know.

It's time Annie. God was telling her to prepare again. To get her house in order. It was going to happen soon. And, while Annie might have fought the good fight and looked forward to her rest, she fought the pull anyway. Faith. She would have to trust her baby would be in God's hands. She nodded off to an uneasy rest realizing that truth: coming face to face with one's own mortality was hard, yes. But having the faith to let go and truly let the Creator have his way? Almost an impossible task. A task she'd better come to terms with. And soon.

***

Naomi

"Did you make the appointment with the principal?"

I nodded my yes at Maine's question. My back was turned, but I was pretty sure she caught that since more questions started hitting me with machine gun precision.

"And you took off for the rest of the week, right?"

I nodded again.

"We're doing this today right? Can't have my godchild suffering another day with this bull crap."

I nodded and sighed. Because here we go, Charmaine was about to start her rant again, I could feel it.

"I mean, where in the name of Jehoshaphat did she get that cutting crap? Don't she know that when we are hurting we don't hurt ourselves? We hurt OTHER people!"

I sighed again only I had to add, "And we would be?"

"Black people. Black women. Especially us strong ones with attitude."

I nodded my agreement. Maine spoke the truth as far as I knew it.

"Are we telling the cousins?"

"NO," I shouted, turning briefly from flipping the sausage in the pan to glare at my crazy best friend.

I sighed again, catching sight of her teasing grin. And couldn't help the small one of my own. While that wasn't funny, I couldn't help but imagine Elaine walking into my daughter's school and asking for the counselor. Or Michelle, whose temper and willingness to embrace her own crazy had been a pleasant surprise. Or Fred… now that visual had me giggling.

"Where's Destiny?"

I could feel my forehead crease in a frown as I flipped another browning sausage patty. Beyond a text that stated, "Gone home. Love you. Will talk later," I had no idea what was going on with my sister. And since coming home from court yesterday, other than reading her text, she hadn't really crossed my mind. I felt a twinge of guilt tug at me before I shook it off. My sister was grown. My daughter was not. Destiny would have to take care of herself for a moment. My focus in the foreseeable future had to be my kids, plain and simple.

"Uh oh."

"What?" I asked, distracted with lining an empty plate with paper towels in preparation for the first batch of cooked patties.

"Did you call Mama Beck?"

"No, why?" I started the process of moving the patties from the grease onto the plate.

"Because she's here. And from the way she's stomping, I'd say she's beyond pissed."

"Crap," I shouted, nearly burning my hand as I caught the sausage I'd fumbled at hearing that news.

Blowing on my burning hand, I barely had time to turn the stove down and reach into the junk drawer for the burn cream before my back door flew open.

"Hey Mama Be…"

"Goodbye Charmaine. I need to talk to my kid."

Charmaine bucked her eyes at me then sucked in her lips. This was not a new expression. It had made an appearance several times in our lives, usually when we had done something stupid, but I had gotten caught, and a butt whooping was imminent.

And just like back then, Charmaine hopped quickly out of her chair, not even feeling a little bad about leaving me there to die and headed toward the back door.

"Wait!" My mom snapped.

And I swear, it took the strength of Atlas to keep from laughing since my best friend froze, striking a pose like we did as kids when we played "freeze tag."

And my Mama, also not immune to Maines power of goofy, chuckled before asserting, "Come here and give me my hug."

Maine grinned, detouring from her path to the door to where my Mom stood beside it.

They squeezed each other with affection before Mom took hold of Charmaine's face by the chin.

"You good?"

"Yes, Ma'am," Charmaine grinned.

Mama grinned back before turning Maine and giving her a slight push toward the door adding, "Good. Now, get out."

I couldn't help myself this time, letting loose the round of chuckles I'd been holding in.

"Yes Ma'am!" Charmaine loudly proclaimed adding a forehead salute for good measure. And as she turned back to the door, with the same saluting hand she blew me the biggest kiss, commanded me to call her later and flounced out into the morning air.

"You."

I groaned. I was finishing up with the sausage when she'd said it. One glance her way assured me that I was not going to have a peaceful morning before I met with the principal today. I was not wrong.

"Nothing to say?"

I sighed again, after pouring the sausage grease into the "used grease container" on the stove and placing the dirty dishes in the sink.

"What do you want me to say Mama?"

"Um. Hello Ma. How you doing Ma? How's life Ma? You could start with either one of those or all of them if you like."

I grunted. I knew a set-up when I heard one. If I asked her how she was doing, I'd get an earful that started with, "How do you THINK I'm doing since I had to find out about my granddaughter struggling from whatever-big-mouth-told-her?" In fact, every statement that she suggested was a set-up as they would all somehow end up going that route. So, I took a leaf from my three-year-old's book and started with the unexpected.

"I love you so much Mama."

"Really? I'm not sure I believe that. Because surely a daughter that loves her mother would call her and tell her when life is beating her down on all sides. Surely a loving daughter would call on her mother to support her during these times. Don't you think?"

Oy. I couldn't win for loosing, apparently.

"Ma."

"Naomi."

Good gravy. She was mad. The attitude steaming off my name as she spoke it told me just how quickly I'd better make this right. But here's the thing... I didn't know exactly how much she knew. And I definitely didn't want a huge reveal to spill with her already stewing in mad juice.

Alas, my mother knew me well. Before I could even go about settling on a strategy, she just spit it out.

"Big Mama called me."

"Um."

"So, I know about your little 'day in court'."

"Uh..."

"I told you once, I told you a thousand times. I did NOT like that boy."

"Okay...um."

"And you will get to the bottom of this Destiny foolishness. I want to know as soon as you know they have someone in custody. You hear me?"

"Uh huh, but..."

At this point, not only was my Mom firing off commands, she'd decided to take over breakfast. Another skillet and eggs magically appeared, along with pancake mix. All while she talked.

"Now, about this Vic thing you've got going on. Give that man what he wants. He's been waiting for you for years. He deserves his shot. He's a good boy. I always liked that one."

"But I..."

Pancake batter and melted butter had been mixed in a bowl about this time. It was something about the way my mother made pancakes. The smell would aminate through the entire house. Which meant I wouldn't have to worry about shouting down the house this morning at my kids to get their butts moving.

"And I'll say a prayer for you today when you head up to the school. Lord knows I'd better not go. If I get a hold of that counselor, I'm liable to choke the stupid right out of her."

I gave up trying to interject and just grinned. Making myself useful, I grabbed plates down for the kids along with the syrup.

Then I turned and enjoyed the sight of my Mom in the kitchen doing her thing. The pretty sundress that she had on in blue and pink hues complimented her butterscotch complexion. And today she must have woken up early and determined. Usually her silver locks fell free down her back, unfettered by ponytail holders or clips. But today she had them pulled back into a beautiful bun with a gorgeous pink and blue clip above it. And because my Mama had always been about her silver, her earrings, bracelets and rings were exactly that; a few with blue gems but most just plain silver.

My mother was a stunning woman at fifty-two with vast amounts of energy I only wish I had.

It was a little intimidating to tell the truth. My mom worked at the General Motors plant in Human Resources, worked out every morning at 5 am (by walking in Forest Park with her girls), drove Uber on the side and sold jewelry that she made at the Ferguson Farmer Markets once a month.

In other words, my mom was Superwoman.

"Hey Mama, why do I smell... GRANNY!!!"

I grinned. These were the moments that I'd learn to treasure. Connie B., in all her teenaged angst and impatience, never failed to revert to the cute little five-year-old princess she once was whenever her grandmother happened on the scene.

At the sight of my mom, my daughter's face morphed into the sweetest most angelic countenance I've ever seen. She rushed past me as if I were nothing (just kidding, I got to enjoy a hint of that sweet grin before losing her attention completely). I freaking LOVED watching these two at every opportunity.

Connie B. had, upon seeing her grandmother, launched herself across the kitchen in two strides and fell into that waiting hug. Watching them both turn side to side as mom squeezed her and cooed, I grinned harder.

And let them have their moment. Mom would tell you that she didn't have a favorite grandchild as she loved all her grandkids; I would disagree. There was something about that first one that held a special place in a grandparent's heart. While my mom didn't show it to the kids, I could still tell that Connie B.'s hugs always lasted just a little bit longer.

Heading upstairs to make sure Maddie was getting ready for school, I deep sighed and prayed for my family. Things had to be bad for Big Mama to call my mom in. Mom is what we often refer to as the "big guns". If stuff needed to get done and that needed to happen yesterday? Mom was tapped. This was something that confirmed what I already knew. I had a laundry list of things to get done today, and I was determined to see heads roll on at least one of those errands.

Still praying silently, I entered Maddie's room. It was time for us to have a hard chat, me and my middle child. And I was suddenly very glad that mom had popped in and was taking care of things downstairs. One look at Madison's upper arms as she hurriedly pulled her shirt on was all I'd needed to see. Which meant Maddie's morning was about to get serious in a big way. It may be more than she can handle, in fact. But she'll live and learn. And that's what mattered most; her living.

***

Vic

"And why is Freda calling my phone but asking for you?" Vic asked as he got up from the couch he'd been lounging on to hand his brother the phone.

And hid his smile as best he could as Zee stared at it in his hand.

"Zee?"

"Yeah," his brother muttered after clearing his throat.

"Why is Freda calling me and asking for you?"

"No clue," Zee mumbled, finally reached for the phone.

To say that he and Freda Renee' Brooks had what one would call a "checkered" past would be putting it mildly.

Their tempestuous relationship began with Freda leading Naomi's band of cousins in the foray to make Vic regret punching the cutest little girl he'd ever seen in the stomach.

Freda had thrown the first punch and, when Zee had grabbed his leg to try to pull Vic out of the dogpile, he'd become her next target.

And it was on from there. Whenever the two saw each other, they would end up arguing.

Or fighting. Or poking, pinching, kicking, thumping… you name it, they did it to each other.

So, it was with a twisted kind of pleasure that Vic grinned, watching Zee's reaction to Freda now.

After watching his brother hem and haw, roll his eyes to the ceiling and frown, grunt and briefly disagree, then grunt a few times in agreement, Vic was glad to see him wrapping up the call.

"Alright, I'll tell him. And thanks for the heads up. Bye."

Vic reached forward to take his phone back before asking.

"What's up?"

"She says she needs your help to keep Naomi from killing her case."

"Really? How?"

"She needs you to convince her to cancel that meeting with the principal today."

"Cancel? Why? Man, no. In fact, if anything, I'm trying to convince the stubborn woman to take me with her."

"Still can't get her to play kissy face with you huh?"

"Bite me."

"No thank you."

"Seriously, why though? From where I sit, this whole thing needs to be cleaned up ASAP. Naomi and her kids' lives depend on it."

"Freda's not saying that you never address it. She just needs you two to hold off for a minute while she subpoenas the records."

"Subpoenas what records?"

"She needs proof that Naomi was never contacted by the school about Maddie's condition. Freda needs time to get unaltered phone records from the school. Her best chance of getting them unaltered is if they have no warning that the subpoena is coming. In the meantime, she needs you to keep Naomi... occupied."

Vic's arms were now folded across his chest.

"So why couldn't she just tell me that? What did she need to talk to you for?"

"She asked for my help with a different situation?"

"Which is?" Vic asked, grinning as his arms dropped to his hands now resting on his hips.

"None of your business." Zee grunted apparently determined to refocus his complete attention on the work in front of him.

"Oh, but it is," Vic argued, glee pouring out of his voice at the opportunity to needle his brother back. "Anything involving Naomi is my business."

"This doesn't involve Naomi. So, go away."

Vic grinned before heading toward the door. Zee would tell him eventually. In the meantime, he had a very determined mother-on-a-quest-for-vengeance to waylay. And he knew the perfect way to do exactly that.

Chapter 14

Destiny

This time around it was Michael who slammed out of her apartment. And this time around she wasn't all that sorry to see him go.

Maybe they both needed a break? Maybe they needed this reality check of what married life could be like for them if they didn't determine to build a bridge whenever something wasn't working.

She couldn't really say. All she knew was that, sitting here alone in the police station parking lot, she felt all kinds of stupid.

Energized by her pending meeting with Michael, Destiny had gone home to her apartment to get ready. And it had felt good, being in her own space again.

Located in the historic Hill district, her apartment was more of a duplex. Her side of the cute little bungalow was fully equipped with her own basement and attic. Furnished with a quaint charm and the nicest older neighbor, also known as her landlord, Mrs. Benton, the only thing Destiny hadn't liked about the place is that one day she would have to leave it.

It was as if God had said, "that's enough," and given her the kick in the behind she'd needed to begin taking her life back. She felt this because, not twenty minutes after soaking in her sauna tub and realizing how happy she was to be home, her phone rang again.

This time it was Detective Warren, calling about her case. There were two young men being held in custody that matched the descriptions of the two men in the video. Just thinking about how that scenario had played out had Destiny fuming by the end of the call.

She'd been violated. She'd been put on unpaid administrative leave that she was told would be followed by a termination if she didn't resign. She'd lost the trust of the one man she longed to have trust her with his life.

And apparently, she was done feeling sorry for herself. Because she'd gone straight from being depressed to being so angry, she could barely see straight. All of which meant, Destiny had two appointments that day; a meeting with Michael and a face off behind one-way glass to identify her attackers.

Attackers. Such a funny word for who they were and what they'd done. It was a word that activated that urge again. The urge to write it down. To write a book. To tell the world how stupid it was to believe that she (or anyone else for that matter) had it all together.

As an acclaimed journalist, Destiny had traveled the world. She'd been to Hollywood, the star-studded events and parties, Milan, Switzerland and Brazil. And there was one thing that was consistent in all her travels, a thing that resonated with her like no other truth. The beautiful people lived broken lives.

Destiny had met Oprah Winfrey, Tyler Perry, the Obama's and the Bushes. She'd met icons, movie stars and billionaires galore. And she'd seen the horrors of war on foreign soil, villages burnt to the ground, women raped, and children slaughtered. But also, the indigenous peoples of Australia and on various islands, the simplicity of living just to live instead of to obtain. The love of a village and how interconnected each member of that tribe was. And in all of that, she'd seen more happiness and joy in the lives of those that had very little but worked together, than those that had much and couldn't even trust their own inner circle.

And all of this had affirmed for her just how real God was. Because in a world where everything was backwards, she'd been allowed to see the joy of what living a simple life truly devoted to the Most High would gain any that chose it. Joy and contentment.

Thus, therein lay the disconnect between her and Michael. Destiny's family was her treasure. Her gift from God. There were others, like Lindsay for example, that abhorred their family. Because the beautiful people weren't the only ones that were broken. Big Mama had taught her that.

"Watch out for the broken ones baby. Just like shattered glass, they cut you without meaning you harm. That's why it's your job, even when you're helping to clean up their mess, to wear the gloves and take measures to protect yourself. Injury you incur because of carelessness is a weight that fits on your shoulders alone; and, unless you allow God to take it, will weigh you down to your grave. It's called regret little one. And it's the worst pain there is."

So, when she'd gone to meet with Michael, instead of being happy about his opening the door to listen, these were the thoughts that swam through her psyche. Quips like regret equals pain. Beauty, yet broken. Careful, not careless. My protection, my responsibility.

All an eerie indication of exactly how that meeting would go.

It had been a nightmare. It had been the worst argument between her and Michael yet. And it had been absolutely expected.

He'd opened the door to his townhouse and immediately turned his back to her, expecting her to follow. Strike one.

He'd crossed his arms over his chest and tapped his foot; body language that spoke volumes beginning with letting her know that it was all on her to make this right and that she was to blame. Strike two.

When she'd tilted her head at his audacity and chuckled before turning to walk back out without saying one word. He'd called her a bitch. Strike three.

She'd left because there had been no point. He wasn't in a frame of mind to listen. And she wasn't in the frame of mind to defend herself against something he'd already obviously convicted her of and found her guilty.

So, she'd gone back home to prepare for her next stop, the Northside police station on Union.

Coming out of the shower she'd taken to wash away pain she'd refused to acknowledge, Destiny had almost slipped and fallen in her hallway as she caught sight of Michael standing there, like some kind of stalker freak. He'd used the key she'd giving him to let himself in. And he'd done it quietly enough that she hadn't heard him – an easy thing to do with the shower running on full blast.

"Have you lost your mind!" Destiny winced at her raised volume.

"No, but it looks like you've lost yours. What was that? You just laugh then turn and walk out like you did nothing wrong? What was that about!"

As Michael was now just two feet from her, his face near apoplectic with rage, Destiny felt herself losing it. Because what did NOT happen is anyone feeling like it was okay to walk up in her house and yell in her face. No, that did not happen at all.

"You have two seconds to step back Michael Wallace."

"Answer me!"

"One. Second. Back off or I will reverse your odds of reproducing anything that isn't a business deal."

At that point he must have remembered who he was yelling at. Oh, Destiny didn't think he feared her declaration for even a moment. But when she'd said what she'd said, she'd sounded just like Naomi. A thought that probably brought to his mind every single one of her cousins. A thought that made his eyes nearly buck out of his head before he swallowed almost indiscernibly, before taking a step back.

Regret equals pain.

"Now, let's start with you getting an understanding. You will not ever get in my face like that again. Nor will you yell at me like I'm your slave or servant. I am neither. And I refuse to be treated that way, especially in my own home. Expect that when you step to me with no respect, you will get exactly what you give. I refuse to entertain any illusions that you may have about who I really am. You have mistaken my having your back, your front, and your sides since the moment we went on our first date, for weakness. I am not weak. I am not your shadow. My father showed me the way. A man respects his other half as exactly that. He cherishes the wife that God has given him, understanding that she is a gift and comes with favor from the Most High. So, the next time you want to treat me like a criminal instead of supporting me when the crime was committed AGAINST me, you might want to remember that."

Beauty yet broken.

Watching his forehead, lips and nose curl into a sneer, Destiny felt something shift inside. She'd always been sheltered by her family. Protected. This was something that she knew, understood and made no apologies for. Life was hard enough. And it would get harder. Being made safe by the people you love was never a bad thing, no matter how much others claimed it made you weak.

But Michael hadn't had that. And everything about him including the very expression on his face, convicted her of being guilty. Guilty of having a loving family. Guilty of knowing who she was. Guilty for not putting his opinion above her self-worth.

Careful not careless.

"Your father showed you what way exactly? Didn't he die when you were four? I don't know what world you live in little girl, but this one has rules. And you broke one of the cardinal rules, don't get drugged and seduced in a freaking bar!"

My protection, my responsibility.

"First, while I still love and remember very well my earthly father, I was speaking of my Father in heaven. Though my mother, to this day, tells me stories about how my dad always had a care when dealing with her. How is it that

185

we both go to the same church, have heard the same messages and read the same bible… pray to the SAME GOD, that you don't know His word enough to recognize it when its spoken to you? No sir, this conversation is over. Because second, any person that is foolish enough to tell a woman that she is guilty for being violated, does not understand who God is. At all. I suggest you get back to basics and make an appointment to do so, if this relationship has any chance of moving forward. Now, if you'll excuse me, I have an appointment to keep."

"An appointment? Where at? Another bar? Are there two men waiting for you, waiting to get another taste of you?"

The sneering tone and childish attitude, Destiny could have easily ignored. No, she would have chosen to ignore it and instead, believe that the man she'd given her heart to had had a bad day, was tired, or given some other excuse. But that hurtful comment? Spoken specifically with as much malice as possible to produce the maximum amount of pain? The rose-colored glasses were officially off.

My protection, my responsibility.

Destiny turned, shaking her head, her expressive eyes clearly communicating how sad this entire scenario was. With no other response necessary, she gave Michael her back this time around, walking toward the back of the house into her bedroom where she closed the door quietly and locked it.

He'd let himself in. He could let himself out. And that's what he'd done. Storming loudly around the apartment, making as much noise as possible, he'd slammed his way out the front door. And again, she wondered as, stepping out of the car, her shoulders straightened, and her resolve increased, if maybe this wasn't God's "not so subtle way" of showing her how she and Michael weren't ready to take that next step. Or any step at all for that matter.

***

Naomi

"Victavious Carter, what in the name of all that is holy are we doing?"

I heard a snicker coming from somewhere to my right. Though I couldn't see the chump in question due to the blindfold he'd placed over my face, I had all the information I needed to take a swing in that direction.

The thump and then "umph" I heard after landing a solid hit, was satisfying. Not as satisfying however as say, someone explaining to me why the heck I was being blindfolded and led around like the adult version of pin the tail on the donkey in the first place.

What I did know, however, was that I had two hours before my appointment with the principal at Madison's school. And, while I didn't have time for whatever shenanigans Vic was planning (at way too early in the morning if anyone had bothered to ask my opinion on the matter), it felt good to get away from it all... just for a moment.

Feeling the blindfold being whisked off my face, I blinked as bright rays from the sun created a halo effect so strong, I thought I'd entered the pearly gates.

Until those gates began to take shape. The shape of a giant turtle and snake.

I couldn't stop the grin that stretched across my face from ear to ear. Hugging myself, I was bombarded by memories. Good memories. Happy memories. Memories of my Dad.

Vic's arms wrapped around me from behind. His light kiss on my neck before he pulled me tightly to him and rested his chin on the top of my head ushered forth a sigh that communicated the heavy sentiments I couldn't voice.

Turtle park. As a child, it had been my favorite place in the world. It had been my sanctuary and a place that I could fondly remember a time when I would periodically have my father all to myself. Time had stolen so many details, like the smell of his cologne (though I knew it was Cool Water, his favorite scent, I could no longer remember what it smelled like), the features of his handsome face or the strength in his hands. But I could remember his smiling eyes. And his laugh.

Turning to my right, I saw the swings that he used to push me on. Higher and higher he pushed me, laughingly encouraging me to pump my legs so that I could go even higher.

It was a time when I felt like I could do anything. I could touch the sky or fly away. And no matter where I went, I'd always come back down because my Daddy was there to catch me.

Shuddering to hold the tears back, I managed to speak the one word that stood out among all the others in my mind.

"How," I croaked through a throat clogged with unshed tears. Clutching the strong arms that gripped me from behind I tilted my head back and to the side, compelled to watch the words trip from his lips. Those beautiful, beautiful lips.

The smile that graced said lips was a bit sad as Vic's gaze arrested mine. However, the answer that flowed from them didn't surprised me in the least.

"Big Mama. She told me your Dad used to bring you here all the time. I asked her if there was a place where I could take you to escape; to get away from everything. She told me this place was it. That you'd come here whenever you needed to think. I need you to sit with me for a while babe, to think. To talk. And…"

Vic's gaze had fallen to my lips as if magnetically drawn there. My mouth buzzed in reaction, feeling ablaze from some mysterious heat buried within, a heat that exploded as his mouth took mine.

I had experienced kissing before, I'd been married for crying out loud. But any kiss that preceded this one must have been sorely lacking. Without thought, my body adjusted by turning so that my arm could circle Vic's neck and grip him tighter to me, as I took the kiss deeper. I barely felt his arms wrap around me, pulling me tighter. I lost time, I lost my resolve to keep Vic at arm's length... and I felt like I was losing my mind.

Feeling a tug at my scalp, I hadn't realized that Vic had wrapped one of his hands in my hair as he'd taken over the kiss, burning away my ability to hear the traffic rushing behind us, the blaring horns of rush hour, or the barking dogs that accompanied jogging owners. And until he'd tugged at my hair lightly (I assume to end the connection), something that failed miserably by the way as, when my mouth had retreated, his had followed, licking my bottom lip before consuming my mouth again; I'd been gone.

A second tug brought me back enough, helping me muster up the strength to pull back. Something that may have been a mistake. Taking in his hooded gaze and his expression hardened by passion, the fire spread from my lips to all over my body.

"Baby," Vic had whispered it, but I heard the anguish in that one word. Anguish I was helpless against.

Which meant my mouth found his again, as my hands went from pushing him backward to gripping both of my fists into the front of his shirt to pull him closer. I swallowed his groan and mentally kicked away the guilt poking at my belly, admonishing me for taking advantage.

Sometime later, the laughter of a child shattered the illusion of our so-called haven, bringing a rushing awareness to the forefront as a reminder that we were indeed making out publicly, right there in the middle of Turtle park, before God and all creation.

Pulling away abruptly, I sucked in air, hoping to get some into my lungs while refusing to allow my eyes to rise above Vic's beautiful, barrel chest.

It was the only way to stay composed. If I glanced up and caught that hungry expression in his face again, I wouldn't be able to control myself. And what surprised me the most was my realization that I really didn't want to try.

And hearing Vic clear his throat did not move me in the least. My most pressing goal in the moment became clear. I would just keep staring at the rapid movement of his chest until I could get my body under control.

A chuckle that shook said fascinating chest abraded my ears, giving me the impetus I needed to pull myself "mostly" free from his spell.

"Since something is apparently wrong with your neck and you can't look up, let's go sit on the turtle. Seriously, I need to talk to you. And I need you to listen for me, without interruption until I'm done. Can you do that for me?"

I nodded absentmindedly, my thoughts still a bit hazy. Stumbling a bit before remembering how to walk and move forward, I held onto his arm as he led us to the giant turtle.

In my confusing and crazy world, I didn't know much. But I did know this. My kid needed my help. My soon to be ex-husband needed a solid kick in his junk for daring to even try to take my kids from me. And I was no longer determined to keep Vic and I's "friend" status unimpaired.

In fact, Victavious Carter had just signed the death warrant on his former bachelorhood, whether he realized that fact or not. You didn't kiss a woman like that and expect to walk away undefined. So, that was that. We'd just have to wait until my divorce was final, then move forward.

At least, I resolved that this was mostly the case. It heavily depended on what he wanted me to "listen to uninterrupted". Because I also knew my present state of mind. And if Mr. Carter came at me sideways in any way about my kids and how I chose to handle this newest fresh hell we found ourselves in, my ex wouldn't be the only one deserving (and likely to receive at some point in the near future) a hefty kick in his male parts. Only Vic was right here. In other words, by the grace of God, he'd better pray that I could stomach what he had to say.

Chapter 15

Vic

Watching something he couldn't fathom working behind Naomi's eyes, Vic took a deep breath.

He hadn't rehearsed how he would do this or what he would say. He'd figured that God would give him the words that she needed to hear in the moment. He fully admitted to himself now, watching her gaze narrow as she crossed her arms while taking her appointed seat on the turtle's back, that this may have been a mistake.

He couldn't imagine what she'd be thinking since he didn't even know what he wanted to say exactly, but watching that narrow gaze drop briefly to the front of his pants as her jaw stiffened, he realized that he probably didn't want to know.

Taking another deep breath, he glanced up at the cloudless sky and prayed for wisdom. He knew how Naomi was about her kids. And he knew that he would need it. So, keeping his expression as blank as he could he dove in.

"You are, without a doubt, one of the smartest women I know."

She didn't say anything to that. He just watched her eyebrows go up and her lips purse.

He could almost hear her "Uh huh. And..." audibly since it rang quite clearly in his head. Something that he knew meant that he'd better get on with it and say what he had to say.

Clearing his throat, he realized that his hands had landed on his hips somehow. He was also looking down at the ground instead of directly at Naomi as he'd intended to do. He knew this because there was a very clear smudge on his brand-new Nike's. Feeling his forehead scrunch up in a frown, Vic wrestled with himself to clear away all outward expressions and try again.

Glancing up, he watched as Naomi's arms across her chest tightened (something he tried hard not to see because God knew that the woman was well endowed), and her eyes had grown even more squinted than they had been before.

Dropping his arms with a mental "forget this" (only the word he thought wasn't "forget") Vic moved forward until he was standing right in front of her. Their heights now equal due to her perch on the giant turtle, Vic steadily held her narrowed gaze and let loose.

"Emotion has no place in this war, Naomi. If you walk into that office today and give those people a solid view of the cards you're holding, you will give them the ammunition that they need to make you look guilty. You will kill your case. And you might lose custody of your kids. So, I need you to think and act, not feel and act.

You don't and Madison will not only NOT get the help that she needs, Rodney would have won. And I so very badly need that brother to lose and lose HUGE. You feel me?"

Vic had watched her draw in a breath as her chest expanded. Again, he refused to look down at that chest and watch it expand. He was a man and only had so much self-control in his arsenal. Control that had already been sorely tested by the most heated kiss he'd ever had in his life. Her lips had parted as if she was about to interrupt but he watched her eyes widen as it did so. She must have recalled her promise to listen. But now he was done. And he didn't know exactly what to think.

She sat there in the exact same position, only, now she was staring where he guessed had to be over his right shoulder. She was chewing on her bottom lip, a completely new thing for her as far as he could tell, as he'd never seen her do that before.

Vic didn't move either. At least, he didn't move until her eyes clouded with wetness. A wetness that hit him in the middle of his chest with a pain so sharp, his first reaction was a retreating step.

And then, he was right back where he'd been, pulling her tightly into himself, as if he could somehow absorb whatever she was feeling.

And that's when he was done with this dance around her deciding that they should be friends. And he knew it was done because his next words were literally those words.

"I'm done. I'm done stepping back and letting you be the 'strong black woman,' which, for some reason means to all of you that you must suffer stupidity like this crap Rodney is pulling alone. So, this is what we're doing. You will NOT go to another court appearance without me. WE will cancel this meeting with the Principal and instead, meet up with Freda this afternoon for lunch. I will check in at the police station since I was contacted about Destiny's identification of her attackers yesterday, and let you know what's up with that. Last, YOU will take Maddie out of school and have a mother-daughter day, with just you and her. Counseling ain't always the answer, babe. These doctors are quick to put these kids on medication. Sometimes, you gotta get to the root of the problem, slay her dragons and show her that she's not alone. That is our plan for today. And after we are done with that, WE have some talking to do about this friend nonsense. There is no way in hell you can expect me to stay in that zone, kissing me the way you did."

Vic had been hugging Naomi tight to himself, her face buried in his chest as he'd dropped that truth on her. He didn't know what to expect when she pulled back to look at him.

Her eyes were still wet, but they were no longer burdened with whatever she felt before.

It still surprised him when she took his face into her hands, smiled a trembling smile and answered with a whispered, "Okay Vic."

He blinked. And stood there blinking for how long he wasn't sure. It was her light kiss on his lips that spurred him into motion again. Motion that had him moving forward to turn that light kiss into something more substantial.

It was after a few minutes of time had passed that Naomi pulled back and, resting her arms on his shoulders, her nose touching his, pronounced;

"Though, just to be clear, that was YOU kissing ME like your life depended on it."

Vic couldn't stop the grin that pulled at the corners of his mouth. Kissing the cute nose that had been resting against his, he fired back.

"Uh no, you attacked me, right here in public. Something that was completely unnecessary since all you had to do was just say to me, 'Vic, I find you terribly attractive. I need you in my life. Will you be my boo?'"

She giggled (a blessing that hit him with a pang on the other side of his chest, considering all that she was going through) and rested her nose back upon his before shattering his world.

"Oh really, so that wasn't you that's been giving me the googly eyes since you were eight years old? I plead the fifth on being the initiator of our first kiss, though, from what Annie B. says, it was quite the moment that we were having over an apology bomb pop."

Vic grinned. "You remember that?"

He felt her shake her head, giving him the famed "eskimo kiss" as she did so.

"Nope, but Annie B. does."

"You were my first, you know that?"

Naomi's eyes widened, easy to see since her nose still rested against his.

"I was? Wait, you remember it?"

"Like it was yesterday." He grinned, not able to keep himself from dropping another small kiss on her lips before returning his nose back to hers.

But she pulled back, her expression no longer cute and open. Her eye lids had dropped, and she was glancing down at her side, apparently caught off guard by that last revelation.

"Naomi?"

Her startled glance returned to his. He felt his fists clenching at her sides and braced.

"I don't... Vic. My life is a mess. I... Look, I want this. Not gonna lie to you. Part of me feels like I need this, whatever this is growing between us. But it wouldn't be fair to you, me dragging you into drama on top of drama. Not to mention my messy self. I can't even keep the calendar updated on my fridge. It's a simple thing. Not hard at all. But you need to know this about me before we proceed. Until the divorce is final, we remain friends. Not because of Rodney, but because of my integrity. I made a vow. And whether he honors his or not, I still need to honor mine or else, what am I teaching my kids?"

Vic found himself nodding, though he felt his stomach bottoming out even as he did so.

Naomi swallowed before glancing over his shoulder then back at him. Dropping her arms so that she was now hugging herself, she continued.

"I don't mind you being at court with me. I'd be grateful to have you there in fact. I just need... time, I guess. To get myself right. To get this divorce out of the way. To get my family right. And I can't say how long all of that is gonna take. Are you down with that? Because, you know I understand if you're not, Vic. Straight up, I really do."

"Naomi?"

"Yeah?" she said it, chewing her bottom lip again, something he was coming to realize meant that she'd rather not be having this conversation.

"Shut it."

"What?" Now her eyes went huge just before narrowing again on him, followed by her lips pursing.

Vic grinned. He should probably tell her how cute he found that particular look. Figuring that he should save that info for a different occasion when he wanted to push her buttons, he elaborated instead.

"Shut. It. Woman, I have been waiting for you since you were six years old. Are you freaking serious right now?"

Vic swallowed his laughter as her chest expanded again and her head went back on her shoulders.

She had an attitude now. Which was good. Because that other Naomi, the one that wasn't sure about herself or her worth (and hell to the yes, she was worth waiting forever for as far as he was concerned) was gonna piss him off.

"No, you did NOT just tell me to shut up?"

"What? Did I stutter?"

Vic watched her eyes narrow so tight that he barely saw slits and knew. He knew that was going to be his only warning.

Jumping back swiftly, he barely avoided the knee that was aimed straight between his legs.

"Really?" He growled, again trying hard not to laugh.

Naomi shrugged before a smug look took over her face. Shaking his head, Vic turned to head back to the car, hearing her scramble down from her elevated turtle seat and, from the sound of the shuffle, skip after him.

Which was why he could no longer contain his grin. Despite almost being in a world of pain had his reflexes been a mere second slower, he knew, without a doubt, that he wouldn't have it any other way.

***

Naomi

I rushed into the radio station with only two minutes until the start of our podcast.

I almost dropped the cupcakes that I'd brought for Vic and Tony, my little way of thanking them for whatever it was that they were doing.

And really, I had no idea what they were doing. But whatever it was, our listening audience had quadrupled in the last month. Or maybe it was just because it had been an extremely crazy month.

After my June 5th court date (also known as the day the earth stood still), where all the original drama had gone down, life had taken so many turns that I wasn't sure whether I was coming or going.

Hitting the doors of our assigned casting studio full speed, I joked with myself in my head that it was definitely one of those two options.

Surprised that Maine wasn't already at her microphone, I dropped the cupcakes on the table and glanced toward the booth.

Tony was flashing the "high five" signal meaning I had less than five seconds to get myself situated before we went live.

Falling into my seat I grabbed my headphones and blinked as Tony pointed at me, meaning we were live and on the air.

I was still breathing hard, but it couldn't be helped. I had what my daughter Connie B. called the "chubby girl" run, something our entire family apparently suffered from. And "chubby girl" running full tilt for the 7 minutes it took for me to get from the parking lot, into the building, up the stairs, down two hallways and into the studio was not an easy thing.

"Alright! Alright and Okay! Here we go people, welcome to the official twentieth podcast of Hater-cation for the Hater-nation! Because you like us, you really like us!" I grinned all of this into the mike, watching Tony roll his eyes as he chuckled from the booth.

Since I didn't have Charmaine to play off of at the moment, I had to pull out all of the comedy stops. From what Vic had shared two weeks ago from the analytics and polls he'd been pulling from social media; our audience didn't appreciate our sage wisdom and sound biblical teaching as much as they appreciated the fact that we were... uh... goofy.

I shrugged my shoulders at Tony as he rolled his eyes and continued to tap dance for my audience.

"While my fabulous co-host hasn't made it into the studio just yet, I guess I will share with all of you why exactly, this podcast is so special."

In my head I could hear Charmaine saying, "Do tell, Oh sweaty one." Good gravy, how that woman could manage to work my nerves without even being in the room I honestly will never know.

"First off, not only is this our twentieth podcast, something I've been told is remarkable since many podcasts don't make it past episode seven, but our listening audience has grown from a mere twenty-four listeners from our very first one to over two thousand! Did y'all hear that? I said two thousand!"

Tony worked his magic and cued the fake applause sound effect, giving me the help I sorely needed in Charmaine's absence. He and Vic were the absolute BEST! And I was so glad I went through all the trouble to make those banana pudding cupcakes (and honey, believe me when I say I put my FOOT in those things. I couldn't wait to watch their eyes roll in ecstasy as they woofed them down).

"Second, because of your generosity with the donations, buying us out of Hater-cation swag on the regular and the support from our sponsors; we have been able to make two substantial gifts as grants to Home Beyond Boarders' CEO Christine Carver, their mission of providing affordable housing and entrepreneur programs to our underserved counties. Please, please, please, if you can, find a way to support these types of programs. There are way too many instances of gentrification around our city and county areas. It's a refreshing thing and a gift from God to have organizations like these that seek to revitalize communities' verses forcing the population out and building them up for more affluent citizenry."

Another fake applause from Tony along with the "keep it rolling" hand gesture, made me wish he was in the room so I could hurl a cupcake at his head. He was telling me to keep going and say something funny before I lost my listeners. I know this because he was rolling his hand while rolling his eyes, all during my entire speech. I wanted to ask him if I was boring him, but I didn't have to.

The reason why I didn't blew into the studio like Hurricane Gloria and banged her way toward her mike, sounding as if a herd of horses just stampeded into the room.

Shrugging off her suit jacket (that it was way too hot for) Maine fell into her seat very similar to the way I'd done only moments before and grabbed her headphones.

"Welcome, Oh late and majestic personage that has entered the studio."

"Bite me."

"Charmaine Renee'!" I snapped

"My middle name is NOT Renee'"

"So," I grinned. "It should be. It goes so well with your first name. And it's all Diva-ish. Just like you."

"Haters never prosper."

"That's cheater's hun."

"Okay, I stand corrected, heifers never prosper."

I couldn't even try to hold a straight face after that. What was worse, I snorted right into the microphone.

"Oh, that's attractive."

"Shut up." I laughed.

My eyes narrowed as Tony started rolling his hand at me again. I seriously started to rethink giving him some of my cupcakes. To eat, anyway. Brother might have to clean them off the top of his head though, if he didn't quit it.

Maine, following my narrowed gaze into the booth, grinned and began to do what she did best. Act herself.

"Wow. Is that one of the lollipop guild in there rolling his hand at us."

I choked on my tongue. No really, on... my... tongue. Because it was either that or collapse onto the table in uncontrollable laughter. Not from what Maine said, necessarily, but from the distraught expression on Tony's face. It was a look that meant, for better or worse, the mission had been accomplished. He probably won't be rolling his hand at us anymore, that was for sure.

I cleared my throat of the tickle that still remained from my swallowed laughter and tongue, in order to continue.

"You made it just in time Maine. I was telling our audience how we are celebrating our twentieth podcast as well as our growth in listenership to over two thousand listeners."

"Did you tell them about the grants?"

"Yes, I did."

"Did you tell them about the streaming show?"

"Uh, no. Not yet. I thought that the news on that is currently inconclusive?"

Maine grinned into the mike. It was a creepy grin. A mean grin. One that made a chill race up my spine.

"What did you do?" I asked it, resigned. Because she was setting me up. If she came in here and mentioned this on the air, that means that she wanted to expose something on the air. Something that would be making someone mad. Really mad. And I was not wrong.

"What ever could you possibly mean?"

I grunted. "I mean that you, High Queen of the Most Petty, have something up your sleeve. What. Did. You. Do?"

"High Queen huh? I like that."

"You would."

I grunted again, my only reaction to her suddenly standing in the middle of the studio doing her "Princess Diana", wave like the audience could somehow see her.

"Charmaine..."

"Heavy is the head that wears the crown!"

"Not surprising since the head is big enough..."

"Grief is the price we pay for love!"

"Will you stop with the snobby voice already?"

"Let us not take ourselves too seriously..."

"Are you seriously quoting Queen Elizabeth right now?"

"None of us has a monopoly on wisdom."

And that's when I'd had enough. The surest sign of that being my notebook that flew across the table and, with a resounding thud, smacked my best friend right in the face.

Flouncing down into her seat with a "hrrrumph," I figured her short reign of terror was over. Bending forward to speak my inquiry of her latest shenanigans into the mike, I was interrupted with,

"The world is not the most pleasant place."

Apparently, I was wrong.

Chapter 16

We'd reached the caller segment of the broadcast when I caught Charmaine's creepy grin again. It was a reminder that she'd never spilled about whatever news she planned to reveal tonight on the air. Whatever it was, somehow, I knew I should not be looking forward to it.

"Hi Sandy, you're on live with Hater-cation for the Hater-nation." I shook my head at my best friend who was currently rubbing her hands together like a sneaky villain out of a Disney cartoon.

"Okay so, this is Mia. Congrats on your twentieth podcast. Hope it's your last. Both of you heifers can rot in hell! I know what you did! Because of you, my contract with Purefix for the next three seasons has been cancelled! You think I don't have connections? You think I don't know that, in order to make YOUR deal, you blackballed me? You think I don't know!"

At this point, Mia was shrieking so loudly into the phone that Tony cut her off, most likely to save our (and the entire listening audiences) eardrums.

But I wasn't paying attention to that, I was watching my best friend do her silent evil laugh, sitting across from me like this was okay. My face was so tight I felt like it would crack. One glance toward the booth was all I needed to see Vic's mouth hanging wide open. Tony's was too, just not as wide. His eyes were huge though, probably similar to mine as I stared at Maine in unbelief.

"So, check out this word from one of our sponsors while I get to the bottom of this, folks."

The beauty of podcasting from a studio meant that we could run it much like a radio show. Meaning, we could pre-record our sponsor segments and play them on the air, giving us a minute or so to get a drink or whatever else we needed to do to prepare for the next show topic. And Tony, always great at anticipating my moves, already had the advertisement queued up and ready to go.

Snatching the headphones off my head, I wasn't shocked that I was yelling by the time I reached the end of my next sentence.

"What in the fresh hell did you do!"

Charmaine cackled out loud.

"Maine!"

"What!" she yelled back. I caught the flash of attitude in her eye, but I didn't care. Because here's the thing, my ex's current mistress slash fiancée had just publicly accused us of ruining her career opportunities – a total hater move, something that we did NOT practice or teach. Not only was that NOT fun, it did not glorify God or serve the purpose of our podcast.

So yes, I was ticked. And becoming increasingly ticked the longer it took Charmaine to explain. Thus, her attitude was now going head to head with mine. And historically, that was a sitch that had never really ended well for her. Mainly because I came fully armed with the power of a headlock maneuver that I was not afraid to use.

"What did you do?" This time I asked it through gritted teeth. We had thirty seconds to get back on topic and I needed to spin this before the entire scenario blew out of proportion.

"I didn't do anything. I merely suggested that, in order for us to host Hater-cation sponsored shows on their networks they needed to make sure that their programmers also adhered to the contract that they want us to sign."

"Meaning?"

"Meaning that, if a programmer was say, in an adulterous situation, it would be considered as a breach of the moral clause within the contract. It would not be fair to ask us to commit to something that they weren't holding their current stable of programs too."

"So, while you didn't name names..."

"I simply pointed out that if they wanted us to sign, they needed to make sure that everyone else was living up to that same bargain."

"And that resulted in?"

"Four shows losing their slot in the programming line-up. Including Mia's Model for Christ, modeling program."

"Oh, for crying..." I cut my comment short as Tony pointed at us from the booth, that we were live.

I did what I did best, making the worst of the worst look not so bad by simply telling the truth. But I swallowed hard against the growing nausea in the pit of my stomach as I did it. Because I knew now that, me and my best friend in the world were about to have words after this podcast was over. And not the mock fighting kind of words we usually play at. The kind that was going to piss both of us right off.

And the last thing that I needed in the world was Charmaine pissed at me right now.

As I'd said, this last month had been beyond crazy. And since we were now in July, that meant a few more things that I had to plan for. Like the fact that Vic's birthday was in two days. It was also part of the reason why I made the cupcakes. Hard to believe but true, I knew that one thing he loved more than anything was banana pudding. The cupcakes were an experiment true, but I had no doubt that he would appreciate them. And in doing so, I'd lay the groundwork for the banana pudding cake surprise that I was planning for this weekend. The man deserved a sweet treat after walking through fire with me for the last month.

To recap, I'd cancelled my appointment with Maddie's principal and instead, Vic and I had met with Freda for lunch where I was given my marching orders. I had two weeks to produce all my (and the girls') official cell phone records from our cell phone carrier. Freda would subpoena the phone records from the school as well as all the school's student information system records from enrollment until now. (Counselors, teachers and administrators were required to enter information regarding students and parent contacts into their student information system for accurate record keeping and follow-up, should it be deemed necessary by the state of Missouri.)

Then, while Vic had gone to check up on Destiny's situation, I'd gone to Madison's school and signed for her early release to have some mother-daughter time. Only, it hadn't been just us. Once I'd told Charmaine the new plan, she'd been all over it, insisting that she come along as the "ride or die" godmother.

Which she did. Something that, oddly enough, had me feeling like a third wheel for the first time ever when it came to my kids. But I didn't mind. Charmaine and Maddie had always had this connection. It was like Maddie was more her kid than mine. From the moment she'd been born, Maddie had always clung to Maine whenever she was around. As a toddler, she'd followed her around the house whenever she was over. Psychology called it mirroring. I called it, whatever made my girl happy. Watching the two of them, their heads close together as they giggled about something in a book Maddie had picked out, I'd suddenly felt like, just maybe, we'd come out of all this okay.

I'd had my second talk with Maddie that day, this time with Charmaine present and available to help. And this talk had gone much better. Our first chat had begun and ended with Maddie acting as if she had no idea what I was talking about. Even when I'd pointed out what I saw as she changed clothes, she continued to deny and deflect.

But this time, with Charmaine there, I got the truth that I needed. Some parents would be mad about their kids not telling them the truth but coming clean for others. That parent wasn't me. I thanked God that I had Charmaine as a resource for my kids. Because if I couldn't help them, someone else that I trust should be able to. And I trusted Charmaine with my life.

And then there was Destiny. As in, there was so much going on with my little sister that my head spun just thinking about it.

The first thing was her ability to identify the two creeps that made the video. Unpleasant and harrowing sure, but I'd figured after that happened then the police could go from there.

Only, that hadn't been the case. As Freda explained it, the prosecuting attorney now had to build a case to see if the two guys should be indicted. Which meant that they needed more than Destiny's word which, frankly, carried very little weight since she'd been drugged. A defense attorney could easily tear a case based upon her witness testimony alone, to shreds because of that.

So, not only did they have to compile other eyewitness testimonies, they had to locate the cell phones and submit them into evidence, hoping that there was some recorded proof on one of the devices. When I'd asked if they could subpoena the records from the sites used to post the video, Freda had sadly conveyed that there would be no way to really locate the initial source once the video went viral. Our best bet was to obtain the original device of the recording. This was not good news since they could just erase that data.

And, if Destiny hadn't been through enough, there was what Maine and I had personally witnessed when we'd gone out to celebrate Maine's birthday.

Vic and Tony had also horned in on our fun, serving as our so-called escorts for the evening as we chose to dine at Tony's Restaurant downtown. Something that neither of us minded since they'd also offered to pay.

It was Maine who'd laughingly pointed out a guy at the other end of the restaurant, dining with a blonde that she'd felt had the biggest head. A head that we only saw the back of. A head that, once we could clearly see past it, had camouflaged the fact that the guy seated across from it was none other than my sister's fiancée.

Two things happened when that realization became clear. Vic asked for the check. And Charmaine threw down her napkin, rising from the table with fire in her eyes.

Tony had jumped up to stand in her path (brave of him considering Maine was not a tiny whimsical fairy by any means) while I'd leapt forward to grab her arm.

Let's just say, that when one threw down their napkin at a restaurant like that, people noticed. And when one jumped up out of their seat, followed by two other people jumping up, a lot of people noticed. That said, it wasn't surprising that Michael noticed us by the time Tony, and I had Maine reasonably restrained.

"Let me go."

Charmaine's voice had gone up to the octave that dog whistles use, something that amazed, frightened and confused me all at once.

Destiny was *my* sister. Shouldn't I be the one that needed to be restrained? Apparently, Charmaine recognized no such rules of protocol as she twisted her arm out of my hold and pushed into Tony to move him bodily.

By that time, waiters and a few bystanders had also lent their presence to help restrain Maine, along with Vic, who was the deciding factor I believe, in her deciding to calm the heck down. You'd have to be a linebacker to get past Vic, something that Charmaine was not.

Once she was secured, I turned to approach Michael's table and give him a healthy piece of my furious mind, only to find that he and the blonde had vacated the premises sometime during our "restrain Charmaine" scuffle.

All of which led to me needing to have a chat with my sister that I did not want to have. A chat that disturbed me even more because of her blasé response. A response that had me worried. So worried that I'd mentioned it to Big Mama who'd nodded while I was speaking as if things were adding up.

"What should we do," I'd finally asked, determined to get a straight answer from somebody; anybody at that point.

"Nothing." Big Mama had responded as she bustled around her kitchen, placing her old-fashioned kettle back onto the front eye of the stove.

"What do you mean nothing?" I'd asked, jumping up to grab the broom out of her hands so that I could do the sweeping instead.

"I mean nothing, child. Look, your sister is smart. Just like you. Don't worry so, Naomi. She must make her choices in this life, same as you. And from what you say, it sounds like she's chosen to insulate herself from a possibility that she probably already knew was there."

I'd frozen in mid sweeping motion as I allowed what Big Mama said to sink in. Was that it? Had Destiny suspected that Michael was stepping out on her? That, and a thousand more questions had raced through my mind; all of which had no answer.

And what had surprised me the most? I'd left it alone. Back in the day I would have been determined to chase down the facts. And make Michael suffer for me having to do so. But today I had way too much on my plate and no time for foolishness, mine included.

So, I'd finished sweeping the floor and picked up the trash. Kissing Big Mama on her cheek (with a loud smacking kiss as we'd been taught to do with Big Mama since birth) I got out of there, jumped in my car and headed for my final stop that day, Annie B.'s place.

Annie B had been released from the hospital Monday of that week. Not because she was doing better, but because her insurance refused to pay for one more day on her hospital stay. She'd had two options according to Maine; go into a nursing care facility where, according to Big Mama, hope went to die. Or, go home and receive home health aid services.

Annie B. had chosen to go home. Charmaine had been livid that she had to make that choice. I'd been scared. Because I'd seen this happen before and it never ended well.

Annie B. hadn't been right since the surgery. We all knew this, and we all hated that we knew this. There was a complication this or a complication that according to her doctors.

219

Which translated from doctor code meant, she's old, her body has worn down and we really can't put our finger on what's going wrong.

So, Charmaine and I had shown up Monday to bring Annie B. home with Big Mama coming over to help once we'd arrived. Destiny and the cousins also showed to make sure that we got her comfortable and situated.

As expected, Maine had taken short term leave to care for Annie B. at home as, she didn't trust strangers and I couldn't blame her for that. I couldn't blame her for many reasons, but mostly for the bright lights that had once shown with force from Annie B.'s eyes were growing dimmer by the day.

We didn't talk about it. We refused to acknowledge it. We just showed up, joked and teased her into acting herself, left, then did it all again a few days later.

I'd shown up late evening as it had been a full day. Annie B. was sitting there in her little scooter wheelchair in front of her big box television, slumped over.

Running to her without thought, fearing the worst, I dropped down in front of her chair and placed both hands on her thighs.

Her eyes opened at about the same time that I realized that those thighs were warm and not ice cold as I had dreaded. But, from the dead expression and milky gaze I'd gotten, I was shocked that they weren't icicles.

"Hey there Annie B.," I stage whispered. I didn't know if she was awake and cognizant or still being gripped mentally by sleep. Trying to ensure I didn't startle her, I finished with, "How you feeling today lady?"

Her lips twitched for a moment before a sad smile finally appeared. Recognition lit her eyes and I suddenly felt the room warm again by several degrees.

"Hey Nahmi,-girl. How you doing?"

My hands still resting on her thighs careful to avoid pressure due to her bones being weaker since the break, I smiled back and said my usual,

"I'm blessed in the city and the field Ms. Annie. Blessed coming and going. Just doggone blessed." I grinned. But the pangs in my chest contrasted with the message that my face was sending.

"Yes, you are, girl. Yes, you are. Nahmi-girl, I need you to do me a favor."

"Yes ma'am, anything you need," I answered hastily.

"I need you to take care of my girl for me. Take care of Maine," pausing to breathe, her voice shaking with every word, I felt my heart plummet to my ribs while an acute pain akin to a knife stabbing me right in the center of my chest hit me. I knew better to interrupt, instead I waited patiently for her to finish.

"I'm tired, baby. You understand that, right? I'm not giving up, I'm just tired, okay?"

Something wet hit my hands. Glancing down, I realized that my face was the source. Tears were running down it rampantly. Instead of bothering to clear my vision I refocused through another wave of wetness on that beloved face.

"Don't do that, baby. Don't do it. This is life, Nahmi. Maine refuses to hear me so I need you to say the words when I'm gone for me. Told that girl I was dying. Told her plain. She didn't want to hear. My baby prayed for me like there was no tomorrow though. So, she knows. She's just afraid."

"Please..." was all I could get out. How do you tell a gift from God that, after fighting the good fight of faith that she hadn't earned her rest? How did you tell one of your most ardent teachers in the game of life that the hole left behind once she'd gone would be impossible to fill?

"I gotchu baby girl. I'm hanging on for as long as I can. But the expiration date on this body has been set. I can push for more time, but I can do that for only so long. Sooner or later it wears out, baby. No matter how strong the Spirit that abides in it. Times almost up. Them folks gonna show up when it happens. I need you to look after my girl. Don't let him get his claws into her again, you hear me?"

I nodded, all but openly weeping at this point. Because while I'd had the best parents and grandparents in the world as far as I was concerned, Maine's experience had been vastly different. Many people could tell tales about that one uncle that the family spoke of in hushed tones. The one that no one left their kids with. All of my uncles and aunts were sound of mind so that wasn't my testimony. But it was Maine's.

And with her father killed early on while selling weed to try to take care of his newborn, and her mother, in her grief at the loss had become drug addicted and useless, Maine had had no one to protect her from him.

Except Annie B. And not before Annie B. had been tried and found innocent for assault and battery seeing as how, when she'd caught the fool red handed abusing Charmaine, she'd taken a bat to him and wouldn't stop until he lay there in a pool of blood.

Big Mama had told me about that night being the worst night of her life, watching her friend suffer because her own son had been hurting her granddaughter. Big Mama had said that they'd used to say to the kids all the time that, "I brought you into this world, I can take you out!" That day, Annie B. breathed life into that saying by nearly doing exactly that.

Greyson Reynolds hadn't been seen again after that. Big Mama had said that he'd sent Annie B. letters that she refused to read. He'd been dead as far as Annie B. was concerned. Because if you couldn't trust your own family to protect you, then who could you trust?

I'd left Annie B.'s house so depleted, so worn out, that I don't know how long I sat in my car on that street without moving.

Having laid my head on the steering wheel I tried to get air into my lungs until huge, gulping gasps were all I could take. When I could finally breathe, I'd prayed hard, I'd prayed loud and I'd prayed long.

Then I cleaned up my face, started my car and headed home to hug on my kids and love on them with everything in me.

That had all happened in one day. And, while the rest of that week had seemed anticlimactic in comparison, the month had been rampant with struggle. From my caseloads at work to my pushing down the knowledge that I refused to acknowledge, that my best friend was about to lose the most important person in her life. A loss that might open the door to the one person that had hurt her the most.

Remembering all of this as I went through the motions to finish up the podcast, I decided to hold off on having those words for now. I needed to get some wise counsel on this, and I needed it stat.

And I would. Therefore, I packed all that drama away again into the back of my mind and watched as Vic's world lit up the minute he bit into one of my cupcakes. I grinned in response to his body literally shivering with pleasure as his eyes closed to surf the wave of all that goodness.

Yeah. I did that. And I was determined to live in that moment and enjoy it. I was learning faster than I really wanted to that life was much too short to let just one moment like this slip past. Grinning harder, I milked it for all it was worth. And I'm glad I did. Because life being the butthead that it was, transitioned from bad to worse at the speed of light. Something that shouldn't have surprised me, but it did.

Chapter 17

My forehead hit the table again. This had become my regular posture whenever I happened to visit Big Mama these days. Because, again, my cousins, through some weird sixth sense, always seemed to know when I'd be there and show up moments later.

And this was no exaggeration either. Within 5 minutes of my hitting Big Mama's door, it was like a Naomi slash bat signal shone over head as, either Michelle or Fred would come waltzing through. And usually, within the next ten minutes the rest of the crew would be gathered around the table.

It was border line creepy is what it was. And, when life hadn't all but lost its mind, I promised myself to have a talk about this weirdness with Big Mama.

But life had lost its mind. And everyone else apparently. I knew this because I'd gotten off the phone this morning with the Dean of Student's at Connie B.'s school, Ms. Kuhlmann. I was one of those parents that took advantage of the programs where my kids could remain enrolled in school all year round. This allowed them to take extended breaks throughout the year for family vacations and such without losing the information they'd acquired over a long summer break. I was a huge fan of the extended school year and had never regretting having my kids be a part of such a program. Until today.

"Hey Ms. Naomi," she'd greeted me. A familiar greeting yes, but then, she'd known me forever as I'd coached her middle school team when I'd been a college student, working on community service hours.

"Hey Mickey Mouse," I'd grinned. It had been her nick name on the squad as a kid. She always wore these two giant puff balls on the side of her head to practice. A bright kid that was quick on her feet and with a great smile, I hadn't been surprised in the least to see education administration as a chosen profession.

"So, don't get mad." She started with, something I never understood. I wanted to tell her that, if you tell me not to get mad, logic says that, whatever it is you're about it say is pretty much guaranteed to push my buttons. But I didn't. Instead, I took a breath and asked, resignedly into my phone speaker,

"What happened?"

"Um. Okay. Well, I should probably let Connie explain her side before I give you the details."

And just like that my blood ran cold in my veins. My Connie was a straight A, straight laced student. When I say that her discipline record from elementary school until now was blank, I mean it was exactly that. So, knowing I needed to brace I asked my question again, this time with firm resolve.

"What happened Mick?"

"Erm. Well. First, she's okay. There's nothing broken, only a few bruises."

"I'm on my way." I interrupted and, not allowing her to say another word, I disconnected the call. Because the minute you tell me that my kid was not hurt but hurt? Nope. I needed to see that for myself.

I barely managed to call Vic along the way to leave a voice mail of where I was going. Seeing as how we'd scheduled an "outing" of sorts at the Forest Park to catch a movie showing on Art Hill that would include me and the kids, I figured I better give him a heads up that things might be delayed.

Texting my supervisor briefly of the emergency at my daughter's school, I rushed into the lobby and made my way to the front office where the Dean of Student's office was located.

"She's expecting you Mrs. Carmichael, I mean, Ms. Brooks. Go right on in."

I didn't register the secretary's gaffe on my name and really, it wouldn't have bothered me if I had. I understood that change was hard. For two years they'd known me here as Mrs. Carmichael. A name change was not something that they'd remember and incorporate overnight.

Rushing through another set of doors that led to Mickey's office I nodded at the chemistry teacher, Chris Jones standing at the copier. Blonde, broad shouldered and standing at six feet, he reminded me of Jeff Jones, the guy I'd gone to high school with. Briefly wondering if they were brothers, I finished my journey into Mickey's office where my daughter sat, ice held to her left cheek bone, her head down as she looked into her lap, and her posture slumped. In that breath I read the tension in the room that did not speak of good things.

Again, I was not wrong.

At my audible inhale I watched my daughter's body jerk as her head popped up. Her focus shifted to me at the doorway before, biting her lip, she returned her gaze to her lap.

Not. Good.

"You okay?" I bit out, repeating over and over in my head to myself to keep calm and hear Mickey out.

Nodding without looking up, I watched Connie B.'s hand tighten on the ice pack on her face. Other than her right-hand clenching in her lap, there was no other movement or communication that gave me a clue about what was going on.

So, I turned back to the source.

"What happened?" This time the growl in my voice was unmistakable. Not a surprise to me since I could hardly see Mickey at all now through the slits that my eyes had become.

229

"Please. Sit down, Ms. Brooks. I believe that Connie B. wishes to tell her side before we talk."

I didn't sit down. Couldn't sit down. My kid was sitting there with a black eye or at the least, a bruised cheek bone. Further, each time I asked what happened, instead of getting answers I got more deflections. My patience had run out the minute I'd heard my daughter was hurt. Therefore, I was not sitting down. And I was done calming down; a state of mind that was made clear in my tone as I addressed Connie B. next.

"Spill kid."

"Mama..."

"Tell me now Connie B."

Now she was blinking hard, her vision still glued to her lap. And I was all out of patience.

"Connie B. Carmichael if you don't..."

"Brooks." My daughter interrupted. "Connie B. Brooks, Mom. I'm not keeping his name."

And just like that, the fight went out of me. It was amazing how that, when we were in the midst of the fight of our lives, sometimes we lost sight of the collateral damage around us.

"Baby..." This I spoke softly though I wasn't allowed to finish what I had to say. True to form, once my kid got started, she was gone. This time was no exception.

"I'm in the bathroom minding my business. I told you about Candy McDonald and her 'girls'."

"You did baby. And, when you did, you told me you'd steer clear of their foolishness."

"I did Ma. I mean, I do. At least until today. She came to school today looking for me, asking around the school for me. I don't even know her Mama. I don't even like her. So, when they..."

"Who is they?"

"Marybeth and Donna, my friends. When they told me that she was walking around asking about me, I just ignored it."

"Good girl."

"So, I was in the bathroom not bothering anybody. I turned from the sink where I'd just washed my hands and almost ran face first into Candy. I stepped back, apologized and tried to go around her, only to have her friend step in my way."

I felt my face grow hot. I tried hard to loosen up my hands, but I could feel my nails digging further into the meat of my palms as Connie continued.

"I said excuse me and tried to go around her when Candy pushed me back."

"She pushed you?" I clarified through gritted teeth. Bruises in the face didn't usually result from just a push so obviously Connie wasn't done.

231

"Yes ma'am. Then she got into my face and asked me if I was the H word."

My eyebrows shot up. "The H word?"

"I believe she means lady of the night, Ms. Brooks," Mickey interjected.

"Got it," I gritted out and waited for Connie to continue.

"I told her to get out of my face and that I wasn't anything. Then she said that she figured I was, seeing as my aunt Destiny was one and that my mother was one too. I didn't hit her then Ma, I promise. I just looked at her and told her again to get out of my face. She pushed me again and asked me if I knew how she knew my Mom was an H word too. I told her not to touch me anymore. She pushed me again and said that she knew my mom was an H word because my Dad found out how much of a who... An H word she was, which was why he left and why he had it much better since he was now dating her aunt. She tried to push me again, but I was fed up with it, Ma. I caught her hand and like you taught us, twisted her finger and bent her arm back. I pushed her away, didn't even hurt her. I just pushed her away and told her I said not to touch me. That's when her friend reached over her shoulder and hit me in the face. So, I..."

Connie B. didn't have to finish. Because I'd taught my kids self-defense just like my mom had taught me. And, even if the odds were three on one, Connie was tall like her dad and me. Physically built to excel in sports with long legs and a strong frame, martial arts and self-defense had come naturally to her. Meaning, unless it was six people in that room, my daughter probably whooped all their buts. Something that Mickey (though her face was serious, I could see that her eyes were glinting with laughter) confirmed.

"I'll finish from here Connie. Mr. Jones heard the commotion in the hall bathroom and ran to investigate. He had to fight through a wall of girls to get to where he witnessed, and I quote, "Connie kicking tail and taking names," end quote."

I glanced again at my kid. While her head was still pointed toward her lap, I could see her eyes peeking to the side toward me, probably to gauge my reaction. When I'd taught the girls a few defensive martial arts techniques I'd admonished that these were only to be used if they felt their life or safety was in jeopardy. Connie B. was probably wondering if I'd considered this situation as fitting for her response.

It was a question that I couldn't answer because I didn't have one. It was a question I didn't have to answer as the next thing I know, Vic was rushing into the room.

Coming to a halt a few feet from my chair, his gaze went to Connie B. and froze. Both Mickey and I sat there dumfounded. Vic's expression had hardened drastically, going from his eyebrows raised in worry and concern to his jaw clenched and eyes narrowed with suppressed rage. My breath caught on the inhale as, on my grandfather's grave, I'd never seen a look so sinister grace his features in all my life.

Next thing I knew, Connie B. was retelling her story and doing it so fast that she sounded like one of those sound machines that made people talk like Alvin and the Chipmunks.

And by the time she was done, Vic had not moved but his expression had vastly changed to smug with varying touches of anger around the edges. I was so fascinated by all of that, Mickey had to call my name twice to get my attention.

"Yeah," I answered throatily; my gaze unable to stay away from Vic who had finally moved to stand behind Connie B.s chair where his hands were now resting on the back of. He briefly reached forward to squeeze her shoulder reassuringly before fixing a razor-sharp gaze onto Mickey.

Obviously flustered at his sudden intensity, Mickey stuttered, took a calming breath and then continued.

"Though Connie didn't initiate the confrontation, she was actively involved and witnessed by a faculty member beyond protecting herself from harm. That being the case, while her initial reaction kept her safe, it is her continuing in the violence when she could have walked away that we need to discuss."

Vic's arms went from resting on the back of Connie's chair to being crossed in front of his chest.

"Um. Also, just so that we are clear, Ms. Brooks, you are authorizing my discussing the details of this situation with mister..."

I nodded at her raised eyebrows and supplied the information she needed, "Mr. Carter, and yes, it's okay to discuss these matters in front of Mr. Carter."

"Good, "Mickey continued, "FERPA laws, you understand." I nodded and waited for her to finish.

"I'll get right to the point. Because this is a first offense, normally Connie would be looking at a day or two of suspension. However, due to the graphic nature of her response, to ensure fairness is observed with a consequence equal to the offense, Connie will serve an out of school suspension term of five days, only to return with a parental conference with myself, the principal and her counselor."

I felt myself chewing on my bottom lip as I nodded my agreement. I know that I should have been angry at someone, everyone... anyone... But I'd taken so many knocks in the head lately that all I felt was numb. Getting my kid home and making sure she was okay had been my highest priority. That and my ignoring a grinning Vic who shoulder bumped Connie B. on the way out of the office, most likely communicating his silent approval.

A situation I still had no clue how to feel about. I was angry at Mia. Angry that those girls dared to put their hands on my kid. And annoyed at Vic who'd proceeded to high five and fist bump Connie B. all the way to the car.

What's worse, when I'd called him later that night to ask his opinion on how I should approach this with my daughter and her father, he'd replied, "Connie B. deserves a trip to Six Flags. And your ex's female needs to be checked. Seriously checked. Something I'm gonna leave to you and the cousins. Because if I get involved, I will ruin more than her career. And by the time I'm done with her and Rodney, she'll wish she'd never even whispered your name."

I'd choked on my next words, words I'd had to swallow as I'd been about to ream him for the Six Flags crack. So, I was trying hard not to fly into a coughing fit when he'd added, "Seriously, babe. Handle it. Don't kill your case but handle it. Cause if you don't, I will. Gotta go, Zee is getting antsy about this algorithm I'm designing. Sweet Dreams, baby."

All of which swallowed the rest of my annoyance down the black hole of me catching feelings yet again for the crazy man.

My neck had grown stiff, but I refused to lift my head up. Because I was here. And surprise, so were the cousins. And, while I didn't need the drama, I did need Big Mama's advice on it all. Seeing as how my frustrating family looked as if they were camping out around us with no hint of leaving anytime soon.

I let go and let God. Well, let go and let Big Mama, to be more precise. And just like I knew that I would, I regretted spilling the beans. Because my family was nuts. And the war on Rodney and Mia had just been officially declared.

C. Marie Evans

Chapter 18

Apparently, time flew, even when you weren't having fun. I say that because it was now the twenty-second of August, a day hotter than the sun itself, and Connie B.'s birthday.

A birthday that I was finishing up some last-minute shopping for before I had to be home to finish setting up for our guests.

A whole lot of guests, too many if you ask me. I say too many because, first off, Connie B.; despite her 5-day suspension, had become an overnight sensation at her school. It was now no secret that my baby knew how to handle herself if someone stepped to her the wrong way. This newfound popularity resulted into two unexpected developments: way more friends than a body knew what to do with, and boys.

Boys that called, boys that texted and boys that came knocking on my door asking if Connie B. were around. Boys that created another unforeseen situation I didn't mind so much, that being Vic coming around to hang out a lot more often.

In the last month alone, my daughter had been on twelve dates. Twelve. I don't think I've had that many dates in an entire year. And every single one of those dates had began with Vic (and sometimes Vic and Zee) answering the door. It was a scene that had cracked Maine and Freda up so much, they started making an appearance on date night as well. By the time we'd gotten around to the tenth date, Vic, Zee, AJ, Maine, Destiny, my Mom, Big Mama and all the cousins were coming around to witness what we now called, "The Intimi-DATE-shun"

It was getting so bad that the cousins were now taking bets and creating a pool on how long each boy would hang around after going through that special brand of initiation.

Fred always bet on the date making one run and that was it. Fred had won every single bet. Something that had irritated Connie B. to no end. But for me, it brought on a relief so great that I slept soundly every single night.

Sadly, all of that hadn't stopped said boys from RSVP'ing for Connie's seventeenth birthday party bash. A bash we'd argued for a full 5 minutes about the location of. My beautiful, gifted, sweet daughter wanted a hotel party. I'd calmly and just as sweetly informed her that she was out of her mind. I was not only NOT paying for a hotel party, or any venue party for that matter; I was not going to set her and a bunch of hormonal teens up to fail. Which could only mean one thing: A backyard shindig.

Juggling the bags as my cell phone rang, I trotted to the car, clicked the clicker to open the doors, and threw the bags into the front seat so that I could reach into my back jeans pocket and grab my phone.

"Vic," the display read. I felt the smile consume my entire face as I tapped the green phone on the touch screen to answer.

"Hey Handsome," I grinned into the phone, throwing my purse into the front seat as well before falling behind the wheel.

"Hey Baby. What's going on?"

Pulling my door closed I started the car and waited for the phone's blue-tooth connection to the stereo to kick in.

"Grabbing the last of the goodies for the party. What time are you getting there?"

"On my way now. You need me to grab anything else or you good?"

I grinned so hard my face probably should have broken from how big my grin was. When Vic had said he'd be having my back from here on out he had not been joking. He'd run to the store and grocery shopped, he'd taken over the cutting and caring for the yard, and he'd been taking my car in for whatever services it was due for lately, something I hated more than the taste of black licorice.

"Nope, just bring your illustrious self and it's all good," I laughed.

"Illustrious huh?" I could hear him smiling through the phone. We probably looked like twin grinning idiots.

"Yep. You shine bright like a cubic zirconia," I added, no longer able to hold my laugh in.

His chuckles eclipsed mine before he promised to see me in a few and dropped the connection.

I intentionally took my time getting home so that I could have some alone time with God, something I desperately needed. I needed more strength from our connection. And to express my gratitude. Because, while my plate was more than full, I couldn't help but be grateful for the people He'd placed in my life.

Charmaine had taken to spending a lot of quality time with my Maddie. We were making massive progress with the cutting thing. Finding a vetted Christian counseling service that specialized in children's counseling had been the hardest part, because Vic was right. At least two of the four counseling agencies that I'd spoken with outlined their method of care, a method that usually included medicating their patients.

So, after a lot of digging, we finally settled on Celine Baltimore-Sampson, a Licensed Clinical Social Worker that came highly recommended by one of Mom's friends. A bonus had been discovering that Celine had a daughter around the same age as Maddie. The kids had apparently met and hit if off, birthing a new friendship. This was beyond exciting for Maddie who'd had a falling out with her best friend Bethany recently for some unknown (but probably goofy) reason.

While I hadn't heard from Rodney or Mia (though, make no mistake, I was still miffed that Mia's niece came at my daughter sideways, never mind that she got her behind handed to her as an end result), things were far from settled. I did, however, pray daily that the cousins would be so distracted by living their own lives that they'd forget those two even existed. Something told me not to hold my breath on that one.

Suffice it to say, I'd been uber busy lately and my God time had taken the hit. I was seriously depleted spiritually in a time when I needed to draw on His wisdom and leading the most. So, I was taking this moment to get some communion in. It was during these times, when it was just me and the Most-High, that I felt eclipsed and overwhelmed by just how great He was... and how small I was. How He sees everything, and I can't even see around the corner. During these times I could do nothing less than marvel at His elegant and powerful nature. Nature that possessed a love so astounding and real that I was helpless to do anything but worship in its grip.

I thought about where He'd brought me from and how, despite my many mistakes, He'd always maneuvered me to come out on top. And I thought about Annie B. She was still hanging on like she promised. But she was suffering too. I watched as her emaciation began to eat away at Maine, helplessly. I could do absolutely nothing while I sat and witnessed two people that I loved more than air almost, suffer. Another reason why I appreciated my time with my King. I didn't have the answers or the power. He did. I didn't have an awareness of what's to come and what is right, but He does. And I didn't have the answers, the solutions or the healing to fix this problem. But He did. And so, as I finished up my private time of worship and prayer, I released all that pain into His hands. Because I couldn't handle it. But He could.

***

Freda

"No, no, no. Move the table over there, closer to the couches. That way the kids can put their plates down on the table instead of on the ground."

Watching Zee grit his teeth as he picked up the table (for the fourth time) Freda worked hard to keep the corners of her mouth facing down instead of up. It was important for every woman to have a life mission. A goal that will keep them focused and satisfied throughout their entire lives. For some reason, Freda felt, down to her bones, that hers was to work Zee's last nerve till he snapped.

Something he never did. A fact that irritated Free to no end. But did she give up? No, she did not. Freda was no quitter.

Watching Zee unceremoniously drop the table two feet from where she'd indicated, she grinned. It was hard to miss that he'd done that on purpose. His passive aggressive statement to her was that she couldn't tell him what to do, he'd never be her beast of burden, blah blah blah.

The calculated gleam shining brightly behind her eyes would have alarmed a lesser man. However, Zee had crossed his arms and raised his eyebrows at her as if to say, "Game on."

Licking her lips and watching his gaze drop to her mouth she slowly grinned. Her very nonverbal way of shouting, "Challenge accepted."

It was a challenge she looked forward to. Flat out needed even. While she was pretty sure that she had Naomi and Rodney's case well in hand and victory was inevitable, there were always the "unknown" unknowns that one had to worry about.

Grinning, Freda couldn't help but recall the Boondocks episode where the character voiced by Samuel L. Jackson explained what "known" unknowns' verses "unknown" unknowns were.

"Simply because you don't have evidence that something does exist doesn't mean that you have evidence that something doesn't

exist... There are known knowns and there are known unknowns – but there is also 'unknown' unknowns; things that we don't know that we don't know."

Freda remembered watching that episode as a young adult and laughing until she was blue in the face. However, just because it was funny doesn't mean it wasn't true. As Samuel J. inferred, the absence of evidence is not the evidence of absence. In other words, just because she couldn't identify a defense for the information that she'd filed with the court yesterday, doesn't mean that there was no defense. Hence the "unknown" unknown part.

Shaking herself out of that bit of reverie, Free scanned the backyard. Fred should have been back by now. As she'd promised, it was his turn to wreak some havoc on the latest offenders against their family unit. He was due to report in on the progress of that this evening at the party.

Free had been sure to keep the wheels of "family" justice operating at its highest efficiency since she'd been unofficially appointed by Big Mama as the leader of their generation of cousins. The Brooks family had several traditions; one being the guaranteed retribution of anyone that wronged one of theirs. And every generation of "cousins" had their defacto leader. It had been a calling custom made for Free.

Athletic, highly competitive and weirdly strategic for "a girl" according to her teachers and classmates, Freda had been groomed for this position in the family the moment Big Mama set eyes on her in the delivery room.

And Freda absolutely loved being that. She got a rush out of the challenge to organize, strategize and wreak havoc where applicable. And knowing each individuals' strengths and weaknesses of their generation of cousins had been the key to keeping that process operating smoothly.

Case in point, the only cousin that didn't get a "turn" when it came to retribution dealings was Elaine. Because Elaine was nuts. And she would do the family no good wasting away in a jail cell. Therefore certain "motivations" had to be put in place to keep Elaine out of the prison system yet free to operate in her gifts and talents. A scary thing really, seeing as how she embraced her sociopathic tendencies whole heartedly and enjoyed people's reactions to them, almost as much as Free loved to plan, mobilize and win.

Catching sight of her brother sneaking in through the side gate, Free grinned harder. It looked like she would be putting her desire to immediately meet Zee's challenge to "do something" off for a later time.

Fred was one of the best when it came to "getting the job done". It was his creativity that she most admired. Rubbing her hands together with evil glee, she couldn't wait to find out how he'd done it this time around.

Caught up in making her approach toward Fred to get all the juicy details, Freda forgot about the eldest Carter brother who was, at that very moment watching her with flamed intensity. A mistake she would have never made had she sensed that he was her most worthy opponent. A mistake she would come to regret.

***

Destiny

Handing two more bowls of chips and queso to Lindsay to take outside, Destiny turned in a circle before grabbing the hot pan, turning off the stove and putting it in the sink. Feeling something tug at her skirt, she looked down to find her very adorable nephew trying to get her attention.

"What's up big man?" She cooed, snatching the hot mitts off her hands, dropping them on the counter and bending so that she could pick up her favorite person in the world.

"Tee Tee DeeDee, I'm hungry."

"Oh yeah," she grinned at the cute face he was making, one that she was sure he knew would get him just about anything he wanted. Especially from her.

"What you want baby boy? You want a popsicle?"

Shaking his head "no" with a little pout, her nephew reached up to clap one hand on each side of her face, squeezing her cheeks as he pronounced with all the weight of a battle worn dictator.

"Cookie."

"A cookie huh? And what kind of cookie do you want, young sir?"

"Want a big deal cookie."

Destiny chuckled, shaking her head loose from his baby grip. In doing so, she happened to catch sight of Big Mama's big deal cookie jar sitting on the counter to her far left.

Her gaze returning to her nephew, she grinned harder before leaning forward to blow raspberry kisses into the folds of his soft toddler neck.

As expected, giggles ensued, making the loss of her shiny lip gloss onto that soft baby skin well worth it.

Pulling free from the chubby arms that had gripped her head, she jostled Daniel onto her other hip and headed toward the famed cookie jar.

"Hey."

The hesitancy embedded in that one word, a hesitancy she couldn't ever remember hearing from him before now, caused Destiny to almost miss a step and trip over her own feet.

Recovering, thankfully, without face planting into the counter; she didn't turn around but kept moving toward her goal.

Mechanical and efficient, her next movements took her right to the cookie jar where she dug in then pulled out and handed her nephew, the first cookie found.

Only, even as his chubby toddler hand grabbed hold to it, his arm had tightened around her neck pulling her head close; his gaze narrowed and focused intensely in Michael's direction.

Biting the inside of her cheek, Destiny turned toward the stove again and moved that way. Determined to keep her calm versus broadcasting the swell of emotion that tried to swallow her whole, she focused on the nonsensical task of checking the foil sealed pots and pans covering the appliance and its surrounding countertops. While that wasn't easy to do since her head was caught in the strong grip of baby Genghis Khan, she tried hard to appear as nonchalant as possible.

"Um. Can we talk?"

Destiny felt her jaw clench tight.

Michael had cleared his throat before he spoke. His former confident swagger and arrogant attitude might be absent now, but his gall at forcing this little "come to Jesus" moment at her niece's birthday party meant both characteristics were just hiding well in plain sight.

Because she'd been ignoring his calls and texts. No, that wasn't right, she'd blocked him as a contact on her phone and on every stitch of social media that she was on. Destiny had cut off every single avenue of communication he would think to use, crying as she did it with only Lindsay there to support her.

That alone had filled her with gratitude, helping her to fight the depression she'd refused to allow to own her. Not that Naomi or the cousins wouldn't have been there for her, or her mom for that matter. Destiny had just felt that it was time for her to grow past the cushioned protection of her family. It was time to stop leaning on her mom and Naomi to see her through. Instead, she wanted to be a resource for them for a change.

And the cousins? What could she say about them? Except what she hadn't needed, which was Mike's brake line "mysteriously" ending up shredded; a mishap that Michelle's first boyfriend had suffered after he mistook her for a punching bag. A mishap that, if Destiny bothered to look, she was sure she'd find tools and gloves soiled with pink fluid in Elaine's trunk.

What she had hoped would happen instead, is that Michael would have some serious "alone" time to think about what he wanted. If he wanted to put himself out there and date again, throwing away everything that they were; everything that they could be, then fine. But what couldn't happen is him thinking that he could have his cake and eat it too. Destiny had no problem knowing that she was worth so much more than that. And deserved the world from her man, the same way her dad had given it to her mom. And if Michael Wallace couldn't see that, she didn't need him or want him. Period.

It was, in that instant, that she was gripped with indecision. Should she give him this? Should she let him apologize? Accept his apology? Or would he just run roughshod over her emotions again like they meant nothing, her starting a precedent of allowing him to believe that a heart-felt "I'm sorry" could get him his way.

For the first time since they'd started dating, Michael seemed to pick up on her turmoil as, he moved so fast to her that it was almost like he'd materialized from the kitchen door to standing a hair's breadth away, his warm breath brushing against her forehead.

Ignoring her nephew's chubby toddler arms pushing at his face, Mike leaned in until his forehead was touching hers.

"Please baby. Please hear me out. I was stupid. I know I was. I'm so sorry Dessie. I need you baby... please."

Destiny's eyes closed, shutting out the intensity of his gaze but not the pain his words caused. Because, she so wanted to believe him. But she so didn't. Not at all. A dichotomy that lanced her chest with sharp jabs of pain. A pain that had been her teacher recently. A pain that reminded her of her lesson of loss, no matter how much she wanted to grab tight hold to her man with both arms; to end both his pain and hers.

It was the shriek of horror that saved her from caving in. A shriek, that married with her nephew's resounding, "NO, NO Tee Tee!" As he pushed hard with both hands at Mike's chest.

A shriek that had the entire family crowding the kitchen, fighting to get in to protect what was theirs.

A shriek that drew Destiny's startled gaze to the back door where her best friend in the world stood, yelling like a crazy person, her furious gaze directed right at Michael.

It was the words however that Lindsay was screaming that caught Destiny off guard. Words that caused Destiny to take three steps back, allowing her nephew to wrap his arms around her head again protectively.

But that beautiful baby hold couldn't protect her from the arrows that burrowed deep into her chest each time Lindsay shouted them. Or from Michael's startled, guilty expression as he took a step in her direction, to do what exactly she had no clue.

Whatever it had been, he didn't get the chance. Because AJ, Vic's baby brother and the biggest man in all creation as far as she could tell, had stepped in front of her, his massive arms crossed over his barrel chest and his legs spread in a way that meant he was ready to get physical.

Then there was Naomi, barging through the crowd with a million bags in her hand, ignoring her baby boys shout of "Mamas", her focus lasered on the shouting Lindsay as she moved in, snapping in Lindsay's direction.

"Fool, cut out all that noise! What in the hell is wrong with you! Shouting down my house like you want the police knocking down my door."

"NO!" Lindsay shouted at Naomi, red faced and apoplectic.

"Yes!" Naomi shouted back, dropping her bags and taking that threatening step forward, a step that meant she was all business and was prepared to shut Lindsay's mouth for her if she didn't comply.

"He doesn't love her!" Lindsay blurted, shouting again what Destiny had heard before.

"He can't. He told me himself that he doesn't even want her!"

"What the hell?" Naomi asked again, only, while her body was facing the enraged Lindsay, her head had turned a near one-eighty, creeping Destiny out a little.

"What's she talking about Mike?" Naomi snapped.

Destiny was shaking so hard at this point, that the chubby arms that had once let her go to reach for his Mamas, tightened again around her neck.

"What. Is. She. Talking. About. MIKE!" Destiny's sister was talking through gritted teeth now, her words a staccato rhythm like gun shots.

"I..." Mike began. But he couldn't finish. He'd been glancing around the room, encountering the gazes of Destiny's family members, each more hostile than the one before.

"I'll tell you what I mean," Lindsay smugly interjected, her own gaze still resting on Mike and more hostile than anyone's in the room.

Then that gaze, full of angry passion, turned toward Destiny.

The crazed expression on Lindsay's face, far freakier than Naomi's neck thing, would have normally sent Destiny running, but the surreal quality of that entire scene had her rooted to the floor, helpless but to hear.

"He doesn't love you, Des. He never did. And I know that for a fact, because he's been sleeping with me for two months now. Haven't you Michael?"

Destiny felt her chest hitch. And, while she didn't feel AJ gently taking Danny out of her arms or see him through the wall of water now clouding her vision, hand the baby to Freda; she did feel the room spin.

When it steadied again, she couldn't see, but felt why it did. AJ was holding her up, her full body weight resting on him as he'd wrapped her in a bear hug; like he was shielding her from what was coming next.

Because there was one thing for certain. Lindsay wasn't done. Despite Vic, who'd also magically appeared now holding Naomi back, she could tell that Lindsay wasn't done. And after hearing what her so called best friend had to say next, Destiny would have given anything to shield herself from what was coming.

"Don't you see Des, I had to prove it." Lindsay's voice had lost its base, her tone now imploring as she took a step toward Destiny and AJ. "You refused to see it. Even when I set up the rape scenario, even now. I see the doubt in your eyes. And I don't get that! How could you doubt me? Me? When I'm the one that has always loved you Destiny. Not Him!"

Chapter 19

Naomi

It was like the girl gave no thought for her life. Okay so, first off, I know that she's a woman, not a girl. But my family had practically raised Lindsay alongside Destiny, just as it did with Charmaine and me.

Big Mama didn't discriminate. White, black, or any other ethnicity; short, tall, thin, fat, it didn't matter. Once you were one of our friends you became family. And, to me, that was not something that anybody should take lightly.

That being the case, to stand there in my kitchen and watch this girl-woman lose her mind and openly admit that she'd set my sister up by giving her a date rape drug? In my kitchen, with all of my cousins present, including Elaine? It was like she wanted to die.

Which was good since I wanted to kill her.

Vic was still holding me back from my current mission, that being to reach for her and snatch her bald. And other than my grunts of frustration as I attempted to do exactly that, a deathly silence had fallen over the room.

It was a silence that Big Mama stepped into, moving toward the stove like she was in her own kitchen and that it was a normal day; not a day when some chick openly admitted to aiding and abetting an attack on one's granddaughter.

And, while Big Mama didn't' seem moved one bit by it all, I caught her slight, almost imperceptible head shake at Freda, who, though she clutched my baby boy tight to her chest, had that look on her face.

Yeah, the jury was in. Lindsay was a lunatic with a death wish.

After reaching in to one of the pots warming on the stove to stir the contents with a wooden spoon, Big Mama calmly turned to face the room with one eyebrow raised.

"Y'all still standing here? We got us a party to finish setting up. You all know your jobs. Let's get to 'em."

And, just like that, everybody scattered. I would have been flat out amazed if I wasn't so pissed. It was my kitchen, my house, and my sister that had been violated. Everybody else could get gone, but I was not leaving until I hurt somebody. And honestly, I really didn't care if it was Michael or Lindsay at this point.

But Vic was of another mind seeing as how, Big Mama had jerked her head toward the door while staring him down. I knew what it meant. And my anger nearly overrode my ability to care about what it meant. I wanted blood. By any means necessary.

Years of home training, however, kicked in with a fierceness that I should have expected. Thus, even while the desire to attack was burning in my bones, my feet followed Vic who had my hand as we walked toward the back door.

I cursed mentally but there was nothing I could do about the little drama that had just played out anyway. At least, not in a way that whatever I did wouldn't blow back on me or my family legally.

And Vic, knowing me better than I know myself, pointed out the little teenaged boy-man that was all in my daughter's face now. Oh, I was still livid. But now my anger had a target.

Marching in that direction with purpose, I couldn't wait to let it loose.

***

It was almost eight o'clock at night and the party was in full swing. It had been a full hour and a half since that mess had played out in my kitchen and I had yet to see my sister's face. What was worse was that Maine was AWOL again. Unreachable by phone as I'd bounce to a voice mail that was "not currently set up" according to the recording, I had no idea where my best friend was. So now I was worried about Destiny and Maine. Which meant that I was more than a little cranky and it showed.

Since my best bet was to avoid conversations with people so I couldn't snap at them, I walked around my yard, taking stock of the attendees. There had to be over forty kids present and I was okay with that since I had a pretty big yard.

Some were playing volleyball on the east side of my property where Vic and Zee had set up a net, and others were dancing in the area cleared for folks to do exactly that with the picnic benches and folding chairs positioned around it.

Tony was deejaying and was doing it well. I knew this because there were always more than a few kids dancing. He was also doing well because he respected my wishes, playing "clean" versions of the most popular songs and avoiding any songs about sex.

Of course, this meant that some of my adult family members were rolling their eyes at my protectiveness, but I could care less. Just because my daughter was now seventeen, officially a driver for over a year now and one of the most responsible kids I knew. She was still my kid. And it was still my house.

Stopping by the grill where Vic and Zee were still at it, I had a quick word with both about how good the meat was and kept moving.

I didn't know that I was moving back toward my kitchen as my body was on autopilot. I wanted to make sure that Destiny was okay. And I wanted to know if dumb and dumber were still in my house. Subconsciously, my body followed the directive of my mind that knew the answer to both of those questions were in my kitchen.

Sneaking in through the back door, one glance gave me the answers I needed.

Big Mama was sitting at the kitchen table, the big deal cookie jar smack in the middle. Her eyes were closed and the expression on her face was pained.

My heart tripped in my chest because I knew that pain. It would be the same pain that I anticipated having one day if I found out that Maine were dying before me. It was the pain I'd felt when they came home that fateful afternoon informing Big Mama and Grandpa Joe that my dad was dead.

Without opening her eyes, as only Big Mama could know, she knew exactly who I was. I knew that because what she said next indicated as much.

"Go on upstairs, child. Destiny's in your extra room, I imagine."

One eye popped open as Big Mama's voice turned stern.

"She needs a shoulder to cry on and a body to talk this through with. Not a big sister lecture explaining how that big sister always knew that a certain young lady was no good... or a certain young man."

My mouth dropped open as my eyes rounded.

How did she DO that? I didn't have anything in particular I planned to say when I checked in on Destiny, yet, what Big Mama said is exactly something I would say (mainly because I was still pissed off.)

I acknowledged the shrewdly shrouded order with a head nod and jogged up the back steps to see my baby sister.

I found her exactly where Big Mama said I would. And, just like when we were small and she had a lot on her mind, she was sitting in the middle of the bed, Indian style; her chin resting in her hands and her elbows to her thighs.

Caught up in the nostalgia of the moment, I almost missed the sound of voices coming from her phone in front of her on the bed. And after listening for a few seconds my eyes rounded in horror. She was listening to the podcast; specifically, the one where I'd mentioned that I hated my sister! Crap!

It was like a slow-motion scene from a movie, her head turning toward me as I stood frozen in the doorway. I wanted to retreat, but I couldn't. I had been given my marching orders by Big Mama; she was not a fan of repeating herself.

"So, you hate me now?

Shock, confusion and frustration warred for dominance over my face. My heart was beating in my chest like it was running a marathon. And all I could think of at the moment was where the heck was Maine?

As if she was reading my mind, Destiny glanced back down at the phone again then, possessing an odd (and disturbing) blank expression asked, "And Maine hates me too?"

When my throat finally allowed words to come out, my voice resembled that of a kicked toad.

"Uh. You ah... you never listened to the podcast so..."

"So, you decided to tell the entire world what you never bothered to tell me?"

Okay, as wrong as I probably was and as uncomfortable as I was in this entire scenario (especially when we should have been discussing the other two jerks that hurt her and not me) I was getting a little miffed. I'm sure that my huffiness found its way into my tone as I replied.

"First off..."

"You've been saying that a lot lately, by the way." Corrected by my little sister in that bland, no emotion tone? Oh, I do not think so!

"So! Like I said, FIRST OFF..."

"And there's never a 'second off' when you say it. It's like you set people up to expect a second point that you never get around to delivering. That's weird."

"Destiny!"

"What?"

"Will you stop interrupting me!"

"But why? It's fun."

"What the!"

And just like that, the sun came out. Not the actual sun, it was almost 9 pm; the sun as in, my sister's smile. Right before she burst out laughing and face planted into my bed, her butt hitting the air while she cackled like a hyena.

Just like that. My own smile was helpless against what I was witnessing. My sister, my baby sister that had been battling depression over being assaulted and losing her job, only to end up betrayed by two people that meant the world to her, was in the middle of my guest bedroom… laughing.

If I had never believed in God at any time of my life, watching all that beauty unfold right before me in the worst of circumstances, a miracle all in itself, would have made me a believer.

I'm pretty sure my mouth was hanging open, even while I giggled. Sounds impossible, I know. But I'm sure my body didn't care.

My sister's head came up from the bed and there were tears on her face. She'd laughed herself to tears. It was like experiencing a rainstorm while the sun was shining. Odd but beautiful.

"Do you know," she pronounced as the chuckles wound down, "that my entire life, all I have ever wanted to do, was be you?"

"What?" I snapped. I didn't mean to snap it, the word just came out that way, like the striking of a whip, it was that precise.

Still chuckling, Destiny was now shaking her head, her eyes to the ceiling.

"Naomi. For as long as I could remember I've wanted to be just like you. You were always so strong, so independent, so… motivated. I've always felt like people just gave me stuff because I was nice or cute. I felt like I never earned anything. And if I didn't earn it, what was the point? You remember what Dad used to say."

By rote the words came spilling out, "Just because you are girls' people will think you're not smart. They'll look down on you like you're small. Remember this: you earn it, its yours. You work hard, its yours. And if they try to take it from you…"

Destiny finished with me, as we'd rehearsed it long after Dad was gone, "You call on me or you call on God. One of us, or both of us, will always have your back."

"What have I really earned, Nahmi? All my life, I've never had to fight because people knew and feared you and the cousins. I've never had to apply for anything, people always put in a good word for me. Even when I started dating Michael, he was chasing me while it seemed like every woman at our church, not to mention others that I don't know about, were chasing him. I didn't earn anything. I never earned any of this. What would Dad say about me if he were here to see me like this"

She was now sitting with her arms spread wide, ending her spate of words with a trembling voice.

And even while I saw her pain, I saw my opportunity. Jumping onto the bed, I knee scooted then fell forward into her spread arms, hugging her close as I flopped us both down onto our sides.

With my baby sister's head to my chest, I started in the way that was totally me.

"He would say, 'you is smaaaht, you is pretty, you is…'"

And again, just like that, the tremble disappeared as she laughed in my arms. Right. I was that good. And having gotten that out of the way, I started again, knowing this time that she would hear my words and my heart.

"Seriously though, Dad would say what I've always known. What you think of as people giving things to you is the favor of God on your life. Babe, God promised that your gifts would make room for you and bring you before mighty men? Do you think it's because of YOU that people see you and go, 'there's something awesome about that girl?' Like Job, you've always put God and family first. So, God put you first. And also, like Job, sometimes we gotta go through crap to understand and appreciate the favor and blessing on our lives. You get that, right?" I felt her head nodding into my chest as I continued, "There is nothing wrong with having that favor on you. And you don't owe anyone any explanations about why it's so. It's a consequence of your life choices to love others more than you want stuff. And that's cool Destiny, it really is."

I paused so that I could look down to see if what I was saying was penetrating.

Catching the furrowed brow and introspective look in her eyes, I finished with, "But apparently you didn't know that it was God's favor and not you. So, He allowed stuff to happen, so you'd learn. And appreciate. Now, your big sister? She's a different story. She wanted to do everything on her own. So, God took a step back and let her. Life got hard but she was a soldier and pressed through, and when everyone talked about her like a dog because of her choices, she held her head high and pressed through. And when the consequences of her choices weren't pleasant, she bounced back and pressed through. It's not that all of that isn't admirable. It's just that, some of it, was unnecessary. If I'd been paying attention, I wouldn't have missed the awesome plan of God staring me right in the face."

At that she grinned at me and said what we were both thinking, "Vic."

"Vic," I repeated, then added, "While I do not regret my beautiful babies being here and how they enrich my life; I know in my heart that their father was not God's choice for me, but mine."

"But what if there's no choice? What if God doesn't have someone for everyone?"

I didn't even have to think to answer, "Its why we have the freedom to choose our lives and chart our own paths. All of those paths lead to our assignments and purposes in life. Some of those assignments involve a partner, and it's beautiful in the extreme. And some of us, our paths don't include a partner; we get to devote all that energy to God. And that's beautiful too. Whatever your path, babe, you gotta stay true to that. What's for you isn't for me. And what's for me isn't always for you. But whatever it is that IS for us, that is what will bring us the most satisfaction and contentment."

"But not make us happy?"

"Nobody's job to make you happy, Dessie. In fact, that's a horrible burden to put on anyone. Happiness is a decision and emotion just like most of them. So, if you can't choose happiness when you're by yourself, how in the world will some other person change that? It's your mind and your emotions. Your state of happiness is your responsibility, not anyone else's."

I paused again to let that sink in. It was a lesson that, if she managed to listen to all of the podcasts, she'd hear again. And it was something I was learning and living, even while I taught it.

Out of nowhere, Destiny was up and crouched over me, bent to kiss my cheek, then bounded off the bed.

"Girl, where you going?" I laughed.

"To start choosing happiness," she grinned at me, again, flooring me with a smile so gorgeous (and so much like Dad's) that I felt a pang in my chest.

"Alright now! That's what I'm talking about!" I shouted that part. And laughed again, suddenly feeling so much lighter, I felt like I would float through the roof.

But just as everything bad doesn't last, good things don't either.

I found that out the hard way.

Chapter 20

Destiny and I were laughing our way down the steps when I heard my middle kid screech that one word in that one way that strikes horror into every mother's heart.

"Mama!" The raw anger and fear imbedded into that shout had Destiny and I now doing something we told the kids to never do, running full tilt down the steps, through the kitchen and out the back door.

Right into the middle of a face off. On one side of that face off stood Connie B. and a few of her closest friends (the real ones, not the fake ones that had found my house just to party); Vic, who had one arm around my daughter's chest from behind, similar to how he had me earlier when he was holding me back, most of my cousins and Vic's brothers.

On the other side of the face off stood Rodney, Mia, Mia's niece, a woman that I was sure had to be a close relative of Mia's — possibly her sister since she bore a close resemblance to the niece, some dude, two other ladies that didn't look like Mia at all, and a little girl toddler that was, at the moment, trying to snatch her hand out of the hand of one of the other women, her gaze focused on the food table.

And in the middle of all that, stood my cousin Elaine. With a plate of food, casually forking into what looked like baked beans and macaroni.

While my approach had slowed as I took everything in, I ended up standing directly in front of my daughter who'd perceptibly calmed once she saw me heading her way.

Momentarily distracted by my one crazy cousin that glanced up, saw me then grinned before beginning to look back and forth between the two groups like we were straight out of the play Romeo and Juliet, I almost didn't notice Big Mama who was standing off to the side, shaking her head from side to side as if to say, "these people are so stupid."

Rodney turned to Mia at his side, whispered something then began an approach toward me. Something I felt shift the crowd behind me closer.

Having to bypass Elaine to do so, Rodney paused then, I guess thinking it was better not to be rude, greeted her in a cordial but slightly patronizing tone.

"Elaine," he said as he took another step past her.

"Butt-munch," Elaine replied before popping another fork of macaroni into her mouth.

Snickers from everyone younger than thirty could be heard around the yard at that one. With one of Destiny's friends laughing quietly behind us and saying, "well what did he expect, that's CB's crazy cousin Elaine!"

271

"You mess with the bull, you get the horns," another friend laughed, causing a fresh round of snickers and giggles.

At Elaine's response, Rodney had hesitated before moving forward with a grunt.

He got up to about 5 feet in front of me before Vic, apparently done with all the suspense, stepped in front of me, arms crossed, face hard.

"What's up, man?"

Rodney paused again, glancing my way first before sighing, he then addressed Vic.

"Mia's niece says Connie B. attacked her at school then lied on her and her friends. I'm just here to get to the bottom of it, man."

Freda, who'd been holding Daniel, handed him off to Madison before taking a threatening step forward. It was clear that when her mouth opened, she was about to let some serious legal jargon loose when Vic interrupted.

"Nah Man. In fact, no way in hell, man. You can't be stupid enough to bring your bitch and her family to YOUR daughter's birthday party, to confront your daughter, who has never seen a day of trouble in her LIFE at school, and you know it. No, you can NOT be that stupid."

Okay, the inhales all around me at the B-word uttered in my yard, notwithstanding (yet something I'd be having a stern discussion about later with Vic), the man had a valid point.

A point that had me settling down from attack mode to monitor my soon to be ex-husband closely to see what he'd say. A waste of time, seeing as how it wasn't him that responded.

"Did you just call me a..."

"Yes, he did, girl he did," Mia was interrupted on a shout from one of the women that didn't look like her at all.

I guess that was the impetus that the only other man in their group needed before he started forward angrily, making his approach.

An approach that AJ met face to face, stopping old boy in his tracks. I couldn't help but grin, noticing the size difference as, the unknown guy, though he was stocky, was probably around five feet ten or so.

To say that AJ towered over the man would not be an exaggeration.

Even saying that, AJ had made his point by stopping the man in his tracks, probably to give him an opportunity to think his next action through.

All of which had apparently been boring Elaine, who, having finished her plate, crossed the lawn like a striking snake, her hand clutching the man's junk and bringing him to his knees with a pair of scissors...let me repeat that... SCISSORS, to his jugular.

As Mia's entire group took a step forward at the threat to this man's life.

Elaine looked up and smiled. It was a smile that made frost run through my veins. A smile beyond frightening that was confirmed when

Elaine creepily loudly whispered, "Come on with it. Come on. Give me a reason."

Horrified, I glanced over to Freda to see if she would reign Elaine in, but Freda was wearing her too pissed to be bothered with getting Elaine under control expression.

A fact that had me swallowing in fear. Because that meant that old boy was on his own. And Elaine wasn't kidding. She was literally standing there waiting for someone to "give her a reason."

"ENOUGH." Big Mama shouted. A shout that even had Mia's side of the party's attention, rather than their guy, who now kneeled with both hands up and sweating like he was running for his life.

Turning to Connie B., Big Mama nodded her forward.

"Say what you gotta say baby girl so this can be done." And, turning to Elaine, she tisked, "Let that man's stones go Elaine! Your kids are watching you. And your baby's crying."

Elaine, still smiling that easy smile, made the scissors disappear so quickly, I had no idea where they went. But she was letting go of that guys junk a lot slower. Like, one finger at a time slower. Which was probably the cause of several nervous chuckles I heard sounding off behind me. Finally done with her display of controlled crazy, Elaine meandered over to one of the benches where her youngest son Thomas sat in his father Andrew's arms, crying.

Grabbing her baby from her man, she bounced the eight-month-old and cooed. "Let's go get my baby some ice cream, yeah?"

"Oh, my Lord." One of the women on the other side of the face off muttered. I hated the fact that I agreed with that assertion almost as much as I hated that my daughter was on the move.

It took Connie B. a few steps to get around Me and Vic, bringing her closer to her dad; something Vic did not like seeing as how he moved to stand directly behind her, his face set harder than it was before if that were possible.

"Hi Daddy," Connie B. said quietly, and sadly, in my opinion. A fact that had me getting all the way pissed again.

"Hey Baby." Rodney's gaze shifted to Vic as he answered. I couldn't tell what he was thinking but I sincerely hope it had something to do with what Vic had said earlier.

Sighing, Connie shifted from one foot to the other and looked down at her feet. Feeling like my baby was feeling ashamed when she had no reason to be, I took a step toward her to end that foolishness. But then she looked up at her dad and I could see the tears swimming there in her sad gaze.

And just like that, I was past all the way pissed off and ready to grab Elaine's scissors from her with my own target in mind.

"First off, Daddy," I heard Destiny giggle somewhere in the background and turned to shoot her the evil eye before refocusing as my daughter continued.

"It's my birthday. You didn't call me to say happy birthday. You didn't come here just to see me and ask about how I'm doing. You didn't even bother to say hi to Maddie or Danny. Doesn't it bother you that Danny barely recognizes you? Doesn't it bother you that I didn't even send you an invitation?"

"It's your mom, baby," Rodney began defensively, only to be interrupted by my daughter's sterner voice, a voice she usually saved for when her baby brother was off into something he shouldn't be.

"No dad, it's NOT mom. Mom has never kept you from us. She never said you couldn't come by or call us. You've been telling that lie to my counselors and my teachers too. But I know it's not true, because mom wouldn't do that. And she wouldn't do that because of you. She wouldn't do that because it would hurt us. And mama would give anything in the world not to hurt us!"

I'd jerked at hearing that Rodney had been spreading that lie to her counselors and teachers. Glancing over to where Free was standing, I saw the calculated gleam enter her eye. And shook my head sadly. Rodney didn't realize it, but by coming here tonight with this BS, he probably signed his death warrant in our court battle."

Probably sensing that, he too glanced in Freda's direction before trying to back-peddle.

"I haven't been saying that baby, I don't know what your teachers are saying but..."

"They're saying what you want them to say, Dad. That they think it's a shame when mothers don't let fathers get involved. They say that you're a good Dad and that you're trying. They tell me that I shouldn't take sides and that both of my parents love me."

Tears were falling now, the water in my kid's eyes having flooded passed the gates as she continued, "But, that's the thing," this she said while sadly laughing through the tears, "you don't. Mom does. But not you. And you know how I know? Because it was Mr. Vic that's been looking through college course catalogues with me to help me decide where I'm going after next year. It's Mr. Vic that has been here for every single date I've been on, giving those boys "the speech". And it was Mr. Vic that took Maddie, Danny and I to the mall last week when Mom was called in on a case and we were bored. You can tell if someone loves somebody because people's love is gauged by where they spend their time or what they spend their money on. You haven't spent time with us. And you haven't given Mom a dime for us. I know that because Mom gave me access to her bank account in case of an emergency, and there has been no deposits, no child support payments, no nothing from you."

"Baby I..." Rodney interrupted but Connie cut him off again.

"No Dad, just... just no. And then, like all of that is not bad enough, instead of defending me against Candy's lies, you brought her and her messed up family to my party." Shaking her head as if she still couldn't believe it, Connie finished him off with, "I'm just done Dad. I will always love you. I will always respect you cause Mom says I have to, but right now, I do not like you. I've already told Mom that I want my name changed. I'm going to be a Brooks, not a Carmichael. Because if no one else will ever look out for me in this world, I know that at least, my family will. Please leave Dad. And take the Suicide Squad over there with you. Cousin Elaine wasn't kidding. All she needs is a reason. And, as mad as I am at you right now, I don't want to see you die."

Turning with her head high, I watched my baby walk away from that with more pride than I deserved. Only to have my gaze dragged back to Rodney, who had reached for Connie B. only to come into contact with Vic, who now stood in his way, before Rodney jerked back.

"Now, " Vic gritted through his teeth, "You give ME a reason. I'm not Elaine. I don't want to kill you, man. I want to make you suffer. You ever, and I mean ever, step to Naomi or the kids like this again in your life, it will be my pleasure to break you off, and destroy everything you love in this world, piece by piece."

Vic was breathing hard as he finished, and so was Rodney. Rodney, who'd looked shocked at first by Vic in his path, was now also hard faced with gritted teeth. And, by the time Vic had finished, they were standing mere inches from each other's faces, freaking me way the heck out.

Until Big Mama almost magically appeared between them with one hand to each of their chests and pushing them back.

Looking up at Rodney, her face sterner than I've ever seen it before, she spoke in hushed tones.

"It's done boy. You made your choice. You and Naomi may have been done, but you still had your kids. You still had us as family. Now you don't. So, gather your people and go. Go on, now."

She'd said that last part as Rodney hesitated. Probably because he knew that she was right. When my mom and dad had divorced, Mom remained a part of the family. Oh, the cousins had a little bit of an attitude with her at first, but they came around eventually.

And mine would have done the same. Because Big Mama would have told them to. But now, after this stunt, he could kiss that goodbye. It was a fact that made me almost feel sorry for him. I watched him come to that realization and, for a brief moment, he looked so much like his daughter while bearing that saddened expression, my chest hitched.

Vic's hand closed around mine. I turned to him, looking up into those beautiful, fathomless eyes and was somehow able to breathe again.

I finally accepted the fact that we would be okay. Not because I could make it that way, but because God wouldn't have it any other way.

Feeling Vic's arm go around me, I turned back to face Rodney just in time to catch another expression fleetingly flash across his gaze. Not just sadness now, but regret shone as clear as day; bearing with it the pain of loss that usually follows. And then all of that was gone as we got his back when he turned to approach the people he'd arrived with.

"So, what? You're just going to leave?" Mia screeched. I hated that she was such a stereotype with all beauty and very small brains. But that didn't stop her from being that as she continued to yell, "So, they get away with hurting my niece? You not going to even address the paint we found dumped all over my car? They spelled my name out with the paint buckets! Seriously! Are you too much of a punk to get it done, then?"

Hearing Rodney growl, I blinked. I blinked because my ex and I had not had a relationship full of blossoms and charm. We'd had our go-arounds , quite a few to tell the truth. But he had never, not in our history of marriage or dating, growled at me.

Then again, I'd never called him a punk. My thoughts were confirmed when he gritted out while getting in Mia's face,

"You started this crap in the first place, you and these gossiping hens talking about Naomi, Charmaine and Destiny. If you'd kept your mouth shut, Candy wouldn't have opened her smart one meaning she wouldn't have had to have her butt handed to her. My daughter does not lie. I know she didn't when you brought that crap to me, just like she didn't lie tonight. Tonight, is my fault. The rest of this crap is yours. Candy deserved that beat down. And if you ever, in your life, call me a punk again, you will experience exactly what that's like."

Done gritting his warning out to Mia, Rodney said louder to the group, "Let's go; and not another word out of any of you. Like my daughter said, Elaine is looking for a reason. If you want to test that theory, by all means, stay. Since I know what was said to be true, I'm up."

C. Marie Evans

Epilogue

Vic

Snatching Naomi into a firm hug, Vic kissed the top of her head, trying hard not to laugh.

They'd come in this morning ready for a fight. It was going to be the court battle of all court battles according to Freda. During Naomi's briefing with Free this morning, he'd been overwhelmed by the energy that Free had been emitting, enough to power an entire substation from what he could tell. Her eyes had been ablaze with some inner light that made him not want to look too closely.

A lover of all sports, Vic had felt an odd sense of Déjà vu watching the ladies prepare. It was the same type of anticipation he experienced, he'd found, when he was about to watch a Venus and Serena Williams match. Not a match where they were teamed up as a double, but the matches where they faced off against each other.

There was always this electricity that was in the air, a power that could be an athlete's best friend or worst enemy... momentum.

And, judging by how Free was that morning, they had the momentum. It was only a matter of time until they had to be in the courtroom where they'd unleash it.

However, that wasn't exactly how things worked out. Oh, Naomi had still won by a landslide, if there was ever a way to "win" a divorce battle. She'd gotten full and legal custody with Rodney giving in without a fight.

Freda had produced evidence that the school had falsified contact records by submitting Naomi and the kid's official cell phone transcripts. And she wasn't even close to being done. After producing written and signed statements from teachers and administrators that were lied to by Rodney, she'd submitted her pièce de résistance, documents that showed Naomi began the filing of Hater-cation for the Hater-nation as a not for profit organization before the podcasts began.

That basically meant that Rodney couldn't get his mitts on any of the proceeds from the podcasts, sell of swag materials, or taxes. Adding all of that to the fact that Rodney hadn't been paying one dime toward child support and his having to pay the full costs of guardian ad-litem fees considering his and the school counselors false claims, Rodney had exited the courtroom with his tail tucked firmly between his legs, something that Vic was all too happy to witness.

And Naomi, her gorgeous hair twisted now into locks and styled into a tight bun, had been magnificent.

The red power suit that she'd decided to wear hugged her curves in a way that was getting him into major trouble. And with her make up matching, diamond earrings at her ears and those glasses with the slight cat-woman librarian look that heated his blood in all the right ways, she practically owned that court room.

And everyone else there knew it too. Especially Rodney who, Mia-less, couldn't seem to stop himself from glancing across the aisle at Vic's girl.

Which didn't bother Vic one bit. Rodney could take a good look as far as he was concerned. Because it was all over. And that meant that it was Vic's turn, making him sure of one thing; he'd never make the same stupid mistake Rodney had.

A vow he repeated in his mind as Naomi rested her chin on his chest and focused solely on him, her arms squeezing him a little, gaining his full attention.

"So, that's that," she grinned.

Vic grinned right back.

"So, that IS that." He repeated.

Standing on her tiptoes to kiss his chin without letting go, she whispered something so small but so significant that it set his heart to racing.

"Chapter two, handsome. You about ready?"

Unable to resist reaching down to kiss her nose, he proudly pronounced what he knew to be utterly true.

"I was born ready, baby."

It was a wonder that her smile hadn't lit up the whole world just then, because there was no doubt in Vic's mind, it had definitely lit up his.

***

Naomi

"Let's go, let's go, let's go!"

I couldn't believe that time had flown like that. In September of this year, one of the worst years of my life mind you, I became a single woman again. And, I honestly don't know why I'd been dreading it. Being a single woman wasn't half bad.

Also, in September, new evidence was submitted to the courts about Destiny's attack. Once the detectives had disclosed to the two men that they knew all about Lindsay's plot, they caved, agreeing to testify to everything in court. Thus, they all pled guilty, saving Destiny the pain of going through a trial situation.

And needless to say, Michael was history. Destiny still battled depression on occasion, but then she'd embrace her happy by reminding herself that it was her choice. In doing so, she'd only needed to apply for one job; a job that happened to be her dream job. A job that my sister got just by skyping in. It was in San Francisco, true. I didn't like that part much. But my sister was no stranger to travel so I knew she'd be visiting home on the regular. Plus, Brenda, her mom, was going with her. She was done with people hurting her baby. She didn't have to say that. I saw that same look in her eyes that would have been in my own. Retired and enjoying herself by traveling anyway, Brenda had been ecstatic at the idea of having Destiny to herself for a while and traveling while doing it.

And now it was a week before Christmas. Life had lost its mind in so many ways this year, it's true, but I couldn't be mad at the blessings that flowed in, despite that.

Like today. We were on our way to church for a wedding. Elaine's wedding, to be exact. After three kids, and twelve years, she'd finally decided to accept Andrew's proposal of marriage, only to spend the next three months fighting his desire for a big family church wedding. She'd wanted to go to Vegas and be married by a Little Richard look-alike. This had not surprised me in any way.

Since my mom was upstairs helping the kids, I was downstairs watching the clock like I was the Time Czar of all power. That said, it was my job to keep us on track. Glancing to the white board on my fridge I saw that it affirmed my desire to nag my family for being too slow. We had a schedule, dadnabbit!

"Coming!" Maddie yelled down the steps as I opened my mouth to yell again.

A little disgruntled, I looked to my left hearing my back door open. And stopped breathing.

Vic had swaggered through that portal as if he owned the room. And honey, him in that tux, head bald and gleaming in a way that would put the Rock to shame, his guns displayed extra nicely in the cut of his clothes... yeah, he did. He totally owned the room.

Shooting that little side grin at me, he did that prowl thing toward me, as was my due. Because I also, was dressed to do damage.

With my peach bridesmaid dress on and matching peach stilettos, I was almost his height. And since the sweetheart cut of the bodice along with the pencil design of the skirt highlighted my curves nicely, I knew that we would make a striking couple. Well, unofficial couple, anyway.

It was the unofficial thing that had Maine laughing at me on a regular basis. Because, to her, it was bogus. Meaning, that we were pretty official in every other way except that "officiality" hadn't been declared.

We went on outings with the kids and without the kids. We had dinners, we went to comedy shows and my favorite of all favorites, we cuddled on the couch in the family room with the kids cuddled up to us while we watched television. At least that's what happened when Connie B. wasn't on a date.

Dates that still drew the whole family and somehow always turned my house into party central for that particular night. It was getting so bad that I was coming to dread the words, "Mom, I've got a date, Friday!"

That's right, Friday. As in, because her dates always caused such a ruckus, I'd limited her dating privileges to Friday nights only. I wouldn't be able to stand my house being thrown into disarray for more than one night a week. And I wouldn't have to either, thank you very much.

Having reached me and bedazzled me with yet another gorgeous smile, I found myself in my happy place. That happy place being in the middle of one of Vic's beautiful hugs.

I grinned recalling Destiny and I's conversation about happiness and recognized the truth. While other people were not responsible for your happiness, they could definitely make it easy for you to choose happy all day long.

Taking my favorite position of my chin to his chest, much higher this time due to the stilettos, I grinned.

"Hi handsome."

"Hey baby," he grinned back. My attention lost in the details of his gorgeousness; I couldn't brace for the kiss that came my way.

And just like all the other kisses that had been coming my way lately, this one was full of heat and about singed my eyebrows off.

My heart beating wildly and no longer having to come up on tip toes to get me some more of that, my hand went to the back of his head, pulling him in so that I could go deeper. Which wasn't very smart considering his groaning response that accompanied his arms tightening around me, bringing my front tight to his.

We'd had some close calls lately and this was one of the reasons why. Why we didn't learn from that and avoid these situations I never knew. Well, actually, I did. It was partly because I didn't want to and partly because I really, really, didn't want to.

From his awesome scent to his phenomenal kisses, I wanted to experience it all in every way. Even when it wasn't wise.

The sound of feet trotting down the steps had us breaking apart trying to catch our breath. His gaze on my lips, lips that I was licking to catch one last taste of him, made his eyes go all hooded before they found mine.

I was sure that when Maddie came around the corner of the stairs, she saw her mother standing there looking nuts, like a startled deer in headlights. That was exactly how I felt.

"Hey mama, Sammie asked if I could come over to her place after the wedding. Can I?"

"Check the whiteboard, baby," I responded distractedly, looking anywhere but at Vic in order to get myself under control.

"Yep, says my schedule is clear today and there's no other family stuff."

"Then make your call, kid."

"Thanks Ma!" Maddie grinned before flouncing out of the room in her peach frilled dress and peach shoes.

Shaking my head, again in disbelief at my cousin that would dare to have a huge wedding the week before Christmas and choose summer colors, I started at Vic's sudden appearance directly in my line of sight.

My eyes narrowed and head tilted. His arms were crossed over his chest and he was tapping his foot. Though his eyes were still hooded making it difficult to discern what fresh hell this was all about, the tapping foot clued me in that it was something I probably didn't want to hear.

"Explain yourself."

And now my hands were on my hips because, what?

"What?" I asked aloud since he probably couldn't read my mind.

Jerking his head toward the fridge, I glanced that way, my eyes no longer narrowed since my eyebrows were probably touching my newly twisted locked-up updo.

"You hungry?" I asked, confusion rife in that question. "Because there's food at the reception, honey." I finished.

"No." He grunted. Yes. He grunted that right at me. Like a caveman or some crap.

"Then with all due respect, at the risk of repeating myself, I ask, yet again, WHAT?"

My hands were on my hips now and my teeth were gritting while I spoke. At this rate I was going to have to put a dentist on standby, I'd been grinding my teeth so much lately.

"So, you're going to act like that's not a thing?"

"What's not a thing?" My voice was going up. Another octave and we'd have all the neighborhood dogs barking in self-defense.

"White board."

Well, I wasn't expecting to hear THAT as a response.

Focusing on the fridge again, I took in the new whiteboard I'd bought last month. I loved that thing. It was color coded with four little baby whiteboard marker slots at the bottom with different colors; one representing each of us in the house. Chores and events were listed in the appropriate color, with a black marker that listed events for the entire family. It was a great system, one that the girls had liked so much that they'd also taken to making updates and tracking new events. We were doing it as a family now and I had been more than proud of my babies for stepping up.

"What about it?" I asked that hesitantly. Did he not like whiteboards? What was his deal? Did he have a bad experience with one or something?

"You don't remember?"

Uh-oh. This was totally me. I was bad at remembering certain things like important dates, important events and just all kinds of important stuff. This was why the whiteboard had been such a challenge for me before, even though I'd needed that system so badly that I'd tried several methods, all of which that had failed miserably.

Blinking, I inhaled sharply as Vic's face was like, directly in mine. As in my nose was almost touching his nose close.

"Uh..." was all I got out before I found myself back where we'd started before Maddie had come rushing down the steps. The kiss that consumed us this time was far deeper than our first go-round. It burned away every thought, every reasoning and every logical progression of information from one nerve ending to the next. I felt as if my entire body and mind had caught fire, a fire that had leached into my soul so strongly, I had no choice but to surrender to it.

And so, I did.

"We're going out the front Ma! Meet you outside!"

It was that shout from Connie B. that managed to bring me back a little. I say a little because I was still caught up in Vic's smell, struggling to stand on my feet even.

Breathing hard, sharp breaths onto my mouth, I focused on Vic's strong lips, mesmerized as they began to form words.

"You told me that you wanted this. That I should wait for you. You told me that you weren't even in a place where you had your life together. That you couldn't keep your whiteboard straight. Since then, you have divorced your dumb ex-husband who I'm grateful to for effing up royally by the way, you have a successful podcast and streaming program on Pure-fix that's going great, so great that you've been able to resign from that good but crazy state job you had, and your white board is organized and consistently being kept up to date. Mind telling me, what the hell are we still waiting for?"

After the longest run on sentence I'd ever heard, I figured it should have been him breathing hard, not me. But it was me. I was breathing so hard, it was like I was sprinting at top speed. I'm not sure if it was because I was still suffering the consequences of that kiss, or if it was because he was right.

Because he was so right. And, I had to be truthful with myself. I was so ready. I'd been ready for a while. I don't know what it is about other people's opinions that cause us to doubt ourselves, but I'd allowed those opinions – the opinions of some older church members, the opinions of some of my coworkers, just people period, to sway me when it came to Vic.

It was too soon after the divorce to be thinking about a relationship, one of the mothers at church had admonished. I needed to take my time this time around, another one advised.

But you know what? What God had for me was for me! And I was taking what was mine. Because I'd been his, the minute he'd stood there in my yard telling me about how he was going to "shoot his shot," and probably even before that, over an apology bomb pop.

Refocusing on that man that I'd made up my mind was MY MAN, this time, I initiated the kiss. And, even though there was a horn blowing outside, and a white board that convicted me of messing up the schedule, I deepened it to a point where I didn't know where he ended, and I began.

"Say it," Vic groaned, coming up for air, his hands clutching my hair. "Say it, baby."

"We're done waiting," I breathed shallowly, "no more waiting, you ready to do this, handsome?" I breathed onto his lips, repeating the words I'd said after my divorce was final.

His smile was so hot that I almost lost the control I sorely needed if we were going to get to this wedding today.

"I was born ready, baby." He responded, just like I knew he would.

And then he kissed me again, and that kiss was so much sweeter, so much hotter than all the others.

And yes. We were late for the wedding. But it was running on colored-people time, so we made it just in time to take our respective bride and groom party places; running as we did so, me straightening my crooked bun.

Not many people noticed but Annie B. did. She might have been slumped over in her wheelchair and looking so frail that she could float away, but her wits were just as bright as ever. I knew that because I heard her cackle as my hands went to my updo again to make sure it was straight.

Flashing her the evil stink eye that basically meant, "mind your business," I almost laughed when she cackled that much harder.

Looking across the way at Vic, I bit down on both lips to keep from doing so. Until he winked at me. Then I let it loose. What could I say? We were at crazy Elaine's wedding anyway. She'd wanted to be married by little Richard so, even though she conceded to a big church wedding, she got her Little Richard look-a-like officiator.

Vic cutting his eyes to the pulpit then back at me had me laughing that much harder. It was going to be a long day. I set my mind to enjoying it. And the rest of my life. Because chapter two was going to be the bomb. I knew this because I knew Vic. And Vic wouldn't allow it to be anything less.

Epilogue 2

Annie B

She could feel it. She could feel her body letting go. And this time, unlike all the other times. She was helpless to stop it.

Her very last thought was of her grandbaby. Her Charmaine. Broken but beautiful, like stained glass.

And before she let her grip loose completely, she prayed for her baby one last time.

Trusting Him, beyond everything, beyond even the unknown. She let go. Her race was done.

Big Mama

Her eyes flew open, her dream so fresh that it wasn't the ceiling that she gazed at. Blinking rapidly, she felt an empty pang in the left side of her chest. And knew.

She'd felt that pang two times before. Once when her man Joshua had gone to be with the Lord and second, when her son was shot. She hadn't been asleep at either of those times, but that didn't make any difference.

Fighting hard to keep down the sobs that tried to rack her chest, Big Mama struggled to sit up in bed. Finally resting against the backboard, she reached over to her bedside table to nab her cell phone.

Pushing the speed dial button for Freda, only two rings sounded before she heard a guttural, sleep-ridden "hello".

"She gone." Big Mama tried to hide the tears in her voice, but she just couldn't. There were only so many pieces of the heart that a body had, and she just had one left. Taking a second to compose herself she swallowed hard.

But she'd never really needed words for Free, her brightest grandchild by far. That was confirmed when she heard her deep sigh on the other end.

"It's going to be okay Big Mama. We got her. Tony and I have had a little chat. He needs to make his move now before we lose her."

"Is it that bad, baby?"

There was a pause that spoke volumes before Freda finally admitted it.

"Maine's been sliding for months, Big Mama. Fred's been tailing her. She's back into that scene again. Girl's in pain, she's handling it the only way she knows how."

"No drugs though, right?"

"No ma'am. Just that club."

Another pause before Big Mama had to ask.

"Naomi know?"

"Don't think so. And I'm definitely not going to be the one to tell her."

"Good." Big Mama breathed. Then breathed some more. Why is it, that when a light was snuffed out in this world, it became that much harder to find your breath?

"When'd it happen?" Free asked hesitantly. She would know that to even think about it was hurting Big Mama tremendously.

"Just dreamed it baby, got the chest pain. Woke me out of my sleep."

And like the other two times before, Freda didn't' doubt that Big Mama was right.

"I'm so sorry Big Mama."

"What you sorry for, child? We all going that way eventually. It's just the one race that, when you are supposed to be happy that you finished last, you suffer all the same."

"Yes ma'am." Freda repeated. There was nothing else to say to that. It was the truth.

"Get Naomi and Tony ready."

"Yes ma'am," Freda said one last time, resigned but as always prepared. "Pray for us Big Mama."

Cora "Big Mama" Brooks closed her eyes hard, fighting to cut off the flow that clouded her vision and responded as she never ceased to respond.

"Always do, baby. Always do."

About the Author

C. Marie Evans is a pseudonym for Chantay M. Hadley, also known as author, Chantay M. James. Winner of the Praize writing contest in 2005, she published her very first novel and has been writing ever since. A jack of many trades - all centering around educating and assisting children - she has also served in many areas of ministry.

Combining her passions of serving Christ and writing, Chantay strives to help others and to be a voice and influence to any and all that can use the encouragement to be all that they were intended to be. A devoted mother of one, she lives in St. Louis, Missouri, coaches Middle School Basketball and loves a good romance, a good laugh... and cartoons.

Author's Note:

I know you're probably wondering, "what's up with all of the pseudonyms?" And you have a point. I mean, how many names does an author need anyhow?

Let me explain.

I LOVE writing, but not nearly as much as I LOVE reading. And there is one thing that I have found to be a universal truth in an avid reader's world, WE HATE it when our beloved authors write into a different genre without warning us!

Right? If I pick up a Stephen King novel and find out its actually a romance and not a supernatural suspense novel as I thought (simply because his name is on it), I might be a little upset. Or a lot upset in many cases.

That said, I love to write. And, while I don't like being limited to one genre, I also don't want to put any of my readers through such an unnecessary trauma.

Thus, following the pattern of many greats such as Anne Rice, I have worked with my publisher to develop a pseudonym for each genre I sojourn into. This way, should my readers decide to visit those "other" books, they do so with full knowledge of the context of that particular genre and know what to expect.

So, if you're into the suspense, technology, scifi and supernatural, the Brainwaiver Series under Chantay M. James will appeal to your love of any of those.

And if you are big on Christian Romance that's not so strict as to be unrealistic but is Faith-based, you will love the writings under C. Marie Evans.

Last, for those of us that find Christian living books need a bit of fun added to them, you will absolutely adore the future releases under C. Marie James.

See? It's simple, sweet and easy. I'll see you soon in the book aisles and, because you may enjoy every single work that's published by MWCP (for which I author many books), I've made sure to list all applicable works under the correct name and in the correct order of release.

I love you all! And please stop by our facebook pages, website or any other social media platform (including Goodreads and Wattpad) to let us know what you think!

Websites: valleyauthor.wordpress.com or www.midwest-creations-publising.weebly.com

Facebook: www.facebook.com/valleyauthor

Instagram: www.instagram.com/chantaymjames

Don't forget to sign up for the Midwest Creations Publishing Quarterly Newsletter on our website!
www.midwest-creations-publising.weebly.com

MWCP UPCOMING RELEASES AND AUTHOR LIST:

Adair Rowan (Sci-Fi, Suspense, Science and Tech)

- Concentric Relations: Unknown Ties – March, 2019

Projects for **Adair**:

- Project Ariel

Chantay M. James (Romance, Sci-Fi and Suspense)

Available to pick up your copy today:

- Valley of Decisions

- Waivering Minds, Book 1: Brainwaiver Series
- Waivering Winds, Novella 1.5: Brainwaiver Series (free for limited time!)
- Waivering Lies, Book II: Brainwaiver Series
- Brainwaiver Beginnings shorts: Wattpad (Chantay M. James)

Projects for **Chantay**:

- Waivering Times, Novella 2.5: Brainwaiver Series (July, 2020 as part of the Anthology WAIVERINGS – will include novella 1.5 listed above).
- Waivering Eyes, Book III: Brainwaiver Series (December, 2020)

M. Renae. (Women's Fiction)

New Author!!! Coming Soon:

- Allowed 2 Cheat

C. Marie Evans (Black Romance and Action)

New Author!!! Coming Soon:

- A Hater's Prayer (July 2019)
- Annie B.'s Legacy (November 2020)
- Legally Bound (July 2020)
- C.J. Series – Action (2020/2021)
  - CJ Run
  - CJ Hide
  - CJ Fall
  - CJ Rise

And many more authors are coming soon! Don't forget to check out the website for author swag, events and giveaways!

Midwest Creations Presents…

Author Chantay M. James and the Brainwaiver Universe!

What if you could have anything you desire? Is what you desire worth everything you possess – including your soul?

Waivering Minds, Book I:
Brainwaiver Series

Celine:

A Licensed Clinical Social Worker in Alton, Illinois, Celine Baltimore lives a content, peaceful life. Until one of her patients reveals that her sister has become a guinea pig for behavior modification technology known as "Brainwaiver," then disappears.

Left with a child's journal that paints her once comfortable life in horror and intrigue, Celine finds herself nose deep in corporate secrets, shifty attorneys and rugged, intense men (specifically Enoch Sampson or Sam for short).

Shocked that she's named a winner in the Brainwaiver contest (a contest she'd never entered) Celine learns of more missing children in Alton and their link to the hip new software trying to take over her life; including Sam's teenaged son.

An all-around goof that can't stop tripping over her Aubusson rug (or keep said rug straight) can Celine let go of playing it safe, fight the good fight of faith and get the guy in the end?

Sam:

A widower and ex-CIA agent turned owner of a family owned construction company, Sam picked up a few skills from his former life. Some he wishes he'd never learned. Espionage and secrets had been his business.

Missions and sacrifice had become his life. Growing cold again seemed inevitable... until he met goofy (and determined) Celine Baltimore.

Could he avoid that place of unfeeling and do the unthinkable? Retrieve his son and love again? Because protecting his family was the only thing that mattered to Sam.

It was something that he would do at any cost. It was more than a goal – it was a promise. And Sampson men ALWAYS kept their promises.

Waivering Lies, Book II: Brainwaiver Series

Max:

Max Arpaio is a Freelance Information Systems Security Analyst and part time Bounty Hunter on occasion. When Max responded to Enoch Sampson's call for help to find his missing son he realized something crucial.

The top government secrets and plots he'd stumbled upon long ago are no longer a shadow on the horizon.

And Now that Denise Ferry has taken up the gauntlet to wage a silent war against Brainwaiver, Max has to make a choice: To help the woman he loves but can never have or stand aside and watch as millions are led like sheep to a slaughter. Either way, he's a dead man. It's only a question of when.

Balboa:

Denise Ferry is a Business Consultant, former FBI agent and a severe pain in Max's rear. A woman who has gone from gang member lieutenant to military strategist to agent, she could write a book on espionage and silent war strategies.

So, when Denise engaged in a search and retrieve mission that targeted children for mind control experimentation, she's in for the long haul to wage war. However, she hadn't counted on warring on two fronts: Against the advances of Brainwaiver and to win the heart of Max Arpaio.

A man of mystery with a sense of doom, Max draws Denise despite her efforts to fight the attraction. Can she help him overcome his dark past?

As a strategist she realizes she has no choice. Without him taking her back against Brainwaiver, she's already lost the war before she starts. And without him in her life she's already lost her heart.

Concentric Relations: Unknown Ties

Psychotherapist Dr. Liam Ronaw
enjoys a rather plush existence until new
client's recite details about night terrors and
dreams. Several dream descriptions spark a
memory from his childhood. In an effort to
help these clients, he follows the various clues
as he works to figure out what connection they
have to his own past.

Dr. Ronaw follows the breadcrumbs which lead him into a world involving a global coverup, a hidden community and a terrible new threat, the likes of which could spell doom for all life on earth.